The Couples

by

Forrest Dunbar

ISBN: 978-1-326-46212-3

PublishNation, London
www.publishnation.co.uk

Acknowledgements

This first book comes with many thanks and appreciation to a few people:

To PublishNation for publishing my book. I will be eternally grateful to you for making my dream a reality.

Thank you Mrs Mary Thorrington, for reading my work right from the beginning. (I still remember our chat about Political Correctness! 'Mr. PC', that name has stayed with me). Your endless encouragement and support has been deeply appreciated.

Thank you Mr Gordon Ritchie, for your tolerance and patience! For putting me back on the tracks when I became derailed. If it wasn't for your brilliant helpfulness and faith in me, Freshers would not have existed in my life. Plus, this book might not have materialised.

A massive Thank You to Dr Michael Faherty, for reading and re-reading my drafts of *The Couples*. Thank you for your excellent guidance and support on the book. You are an inspiration to me!

Lastly, thank you to my Great Auntie Gloria! For listening patiently to the chaotic storyline of *The Couples* before I even wrote it.

Thank you!

To
Mum and Dad,
My Siblings and My Grandparents.

ONE

The main London gangster group are known as 'Fists and Guns', and they were the most feared gang in the world. They were on the minds of every street walker, home owner and police force. It would be common sense not to get involved or stand in the way of any member of the gang as the consequences would be fatal. However, something out of the ordinary was happening. Helicopters were flying over Castle Avenue and camera crews were filming footage that would automatically go down in history. Stowie Parker, London's most malignant, dastardly member of Fists and Guns was returning items to a house that his gang stole from the previous afternoon. Everything was being carried through the house and returned to the exact spot from where they were taken.

A man appeared by the front door standing in a long dressing gown with half his face shaven, his big, orange-coloured, rimmed spectacles placed loosely on his forehead. His bushy black hair stuck up at all angles and he looked confused by this unexpected performance. Stowie Parker approached the man as if he knew him well. The man smiled back respectfully.

"Sorry about all this, Mr Cockflint, if I was aware that you lived here I would have broken into the house next door. I am very sorry for the inconvenience."

"Ah, Stowie, everybody makes mistakes. Think nothing of it."

The two men exchanged pleasantries and went about their daily business. This was reported worldwide and shocked everyone that Stowie Parker the gangster was actually apologising for causing an upset. Newspapers were published in a flash and Clifford Cockflint was being praised left, right and centre.

The Cockflint household had a very homely aspect attached to it, and a feeling of warmth hit every visitor on the way in. Christine, who was Clifford's wife, loved pictures of her family and friends, and their walls were covered with pictures from different eras. The main picture that hung with pride was Clifford and Christine's wedding portrait and underneath was another portrait of their two children, Michelle and Malcolm. All around the house were pictures to remind them of their happy times. Once the front door was shut that sense of warmth filled the atmosphere.

Clifford hurriedly ran back into the bathroom to finish shaving. He had always thought that it was essential to look presentable before breakfast. In fact his appearance was always pristine. Clifford had been brought up to always look tidy and he did that very well, very well indeed, although he did allow his reading and electric train room to get untidy. His wife Christine brought in his bowl of porridge and a pot of tea on the breakfast tray and placed it on the table. Christine had a very warmly appearance about her. She had brown hair that just went beyond her shoulders. Her hair is and will always be well kept. One of the things that Clifford fell in love with was her caring smile. Clifford said that her smile spoke to him saying, "I am happy to help people. I am genuine. I love my family and friends." Her speech was soft and there was never an aggressive word from her. If she was unhappy about something (which was rare) then she would indicate the problem. Clifford and Christine are a well-loved, admired and respected couple of twenty-eight years.

The warmth that lingered in the hallway travelled around the house and eventually came to the dining room. Clifford and Christine loved eating and talking to one another in there. That was the only time they really spent any time with each other.

They felt the warmth of the house around them. The glass sliding door that was behind the dining table overlooked Christine's picturesque garden. Christine plants wild flowers and she had hanging baskets that hung there that could been seen from anywhere in the garden. Clifford on the other hand did not have the same passion for planting flowers like his wife did. "Clifford, dear, would you ever plant some flowers of your own?" Christine would say to him. Clifford would look at her confused.

"What? You're asking me if I want to plant flowers? I cannot be bothered with all that shite." Clifford was a kind person but he did have a sense of bluntness when he really disliked something or disagreed with something. His place in the garden was right at the bottom. A big, shabby, white shed stood there, its vintage appearance was what Clifford loved about it. Outside it people could hear the sound of Clifford's steam trains puffing around the shed on a tall, wide table. He had an obsessive passion for trains, and some days would pass by when Christine would realise that she had barely seen Clifford because he was too busy adding track for his wonderful models that were his trains. On other days he would be sitting outside his shed reading a book. It was his comfort zone and place of sanctuary. Even though Clifford and Christine had their own separate corners, their bonding time took place in their homely dining room. A well varnished wooden table rested in the middle of the room and a grandfather clock that never stopped stood grandly in the corner ticking away. The clock belonged to Clifford's father and he was going to sell it. Clifford had always had a love for different clocks, therefore when his father was not looking he took the clock and told his father that a child had stolen it. When his father saw the clock standing in the corner, Clifford said that he had found one exactly the same. Strangely to Clifford his father fell for his trickery. The dining room presented a vintage style but that is how the couple wanted it. They were not materialistic and hated the modern idea of disposing of everything and then buying unnecessary things. Their lives were cluttered enough and the last thing they wanted was for their house to be cluttered. A daily ritual was Christine would make breakfast for the two of them and then they would open their letters together.

Their marriage was not an easy ride as Clifford seemed to get struck down by a continuous streak of bad luck, but he somehow managed to take every setback on the chin. Clifford was a serious workaholic. He was a proud English teacher who strived for success for all his students. Sadly, Christine was diagnosed with breast cancer the previous year but made a miraculous recovery. Her illness seriously affected Clifford's state of mind and he took some time off work because Christine undertook surgery and she needed him to care for her. He came to realise, after many hours of consideration, that he had neglected her and spent more of his time reading Dickens to an ungrateful class rather than spending time with his caring, tolerant and loving wife. After Clifford discussed his problems with the headmaster, Rufus Feldman, they arranged an agreement that Clifford was to take a year out and spend time with Christine. Christine, however, continued her work as she worked from home anyway. She was a psychiatrist who helped troubled patients about their marriage, family relations and stress.

"Oh dear, Christine," said Clifford, adding masses of sugar to his porridge then majestically mixing it before taking the first spoonful. "Stowie and his gentlemen companions accidentally thought our house was Rufus's house."

"What do they want Rufus for?" asked Christine curiously.

"Well, their Jewish home is full of expensive items. Stowie's satellite navigation device did not state clearly which house was his, and as we live next door I suppose they took a lucky guess, which then turned out to be not so lucky."

"Oh well, that explains it then, dear," replied Christine.

As the pair ate their breakfast they opened the post. "Once again, Christine, I have received David Beckham's fan mail and David Cameron's hate mail." There was a package for David Cameron but Clifford always opened it. He thought what David Cameron did not know could not harm him. Clifford stuck his left hand into the package and pulled out a massive blob of faeces.

"Argh!" shouted Christine jumping up from her chair. "Get rid of that disgusting box now! I do not want that up on the dining table. Dispose of it at once!" It was a rarity for Christine to get agitated as she was a very tranquil person. Nothing ever seemed to irritate her and she took everything on the chin like Clifford. Clifford took the box and disposed of it later returning to the table with clean hands. He had used up a whole litre bottle of disinfectant.

"Christine, I did not feel the need to get hysterical as that is the fourth time this month this has happened and it's only the eleventh."

"Out of all the houses in London we are the only ones who get letters like that. Talk about junk mail literally."

"I ring up the staff repeatedly but there is nothing they can do because they don't understand who is posting these letters," said Clifford.

"We can all live and hope that this stops one day," said Christine praying.

They continued breakfast with Clifford eating his porridge slowly while reading the newspaper as Christine delicately buttered her toast. She normally had fruit for breakfast and since her illness the kitchen cupboards and fridge were filled with health food and snacks. Christine had her own section in the fridge which contained fruits, low fat yoghurts and salads. She drank Chinese tea which had given her a new lease of life, but this morning she fancied something different like a slice of toast with butter. "Don't have too much butter will you, Christine" said Clifford worryingly, pausing from reading an article about a father of the bride who ran off with a nun.

"I know it's naughty, Clifford, but today I just want a break from healthy stuff."

"Okay, Christine, but you should be more like me. Eat healthily all the time." Clifford had said that while biting into a custard tart after eating his porridge which he had poured syrup over.

"Clifford, if I ate like you I would have no teeth left." The couple laughed together.

Christine looked at her watch and realised that her first patient of the day was to be at the house in twenty-five minutes. She quickly washed up the dishes and then went upstairs into her office where she would sit and listen attentively to her patients.

Clifford got his coat off the hook and stood outside his front door looking at the houses opposite. It was a typical suburban area of similar houses with similar sized gardens. The young Catholic couple living on the other side were called Simon and Sarah. Their house just happened to be painted purple and that was the only different characteristic their house had. Clifford adored this neighbourhood and never wanted to leave. Meanwhile Clifford got his car out to take Rufus Feldman, his Jewish neighbour, to work. Rufus was known by the community as 'DOR' (which stood for Do One Rufus). People disliked Rufus as they never saw him in a positive light. Clifford and Christine managed to get past his irritating, very selfish, arrogant, pompous and extremely tight with money attitude. Also he wore very old-looking clothes which looked as if they had been passed down through generations of Rufus's family. Rufus cringed at the concept of buying new clothes and just the thought of breaking into a five pound note made him feel ill. He also had a tremendous nose and if he ran into a wall it was clear that it would be his nose that would hit the wall first followed by his man boobs, or as Rufus referred to them as spare skin. Even though it was a challenge to befriend Rufus (not that there were many who wanted to be associated with him) Clifford and Christine did enjoy his and his long-suffering wife Lydia's company.

However, Clifford and Rufus both do get on brilliantly. They work at the same school and have a very close friendship. Rufus was very supportive towards Clifford when he knew that he needed time at home to care for Christine. They do have completely different personalities as Rufus is a very selfish man and he sometimes took advantage of Clifford's decent nature. The reason Clifford brought Rufus to work was because he refused to drive his own car due to the cost of petrol. Rufus rarely paid Clifford, he did not even buy him a small gift of thanks. Sometimes his wife Lydia would contribute towards the petrol money for Clifford. Lydia and Rufus had been married for twenty-nine years and all was well until about their tenth anniversary when they suddenly grew apart. In the last year their relationship was on the rocks and Rufus began to feel depressed again as the memories of his accident occurred in his nightmares. When he was eight Rufus was circumcised by a drunken doctor who accidentally cut off his penis altogether, but luckily for him another doctor sewed it back on. Unfortunately Rufus was not capable of having children and sometimes when he urinated his urine leaked off the top part of his penis. The problem about him not having children was that he could not get an erection high enough to actually enter his wife. On his wedding night he took fourteen Viagra pills and spent the night with two bags of frozen peas sellotaped to his head in an attempt to reduce his unbearable headache. Also, he thought he had had a stroke as he could not feel the right side of his body, but that was only because he had fallen from his bed. The Viagra pills did nothing for him, his cock didn't expand, the only thing that Viagra erected for Rufus was his hair, it shot up straight and hardened within seconds. Lydia sat on the bed ignoring her newly-wed husband and laid there watching a Jewish version of *Songs of Praise*.

Lydia Feldman was approaching fifty-three. That did not bother her as she considered people old when they reach eighty, but it was the fact that she had started the rocky journey of the dreaded menopause. Lydia had noticed significant changes in her lifestyle. She was suddenly taking pills to help her high blood pressure, something she had never experienced until she hit menopause. Also, around her mouth, thick and noticeable hair was growing. When she entered her en-suite bathroom she would shout at Rufus for not clearing up after he had had his shave but then she would remember that all the hair was from her face. With the amount of hair she was shaving off she could have stuffed a mattress. In the mornings Lydia woke up earlier than she used to because she needed the extra hours to apply her make-up. She would often say, "Oh, I used to be so beautiful, my face was near enough perfect. Now it looks as if a steamroller has run over me." Then she would cry because she would then think of her weight. "Now I am fat and saggy. Maybe it would be better if a steamroller did run over me. At least I would be thin."

"Thin and dead!" was the reply from Rufus.

All these experiences were something that Lydia wanted to talk about to Rufus, but she refrained from telling him because she knew deep down that her marriage had lost its sparkle.

When Rufus would get into Clifford's car and go to work, Christine's first patient was Lydia. Rufus was totally unaware of her private conversations with Christine. Plus the sessions were twenty pounds an hour and Rufus would have hit the roof more about the cost if he had ever found out. "Oh, Clifford, that woman is driving me crazy," said Rufus having his daily grumble. "She spends my money all the bloody time. I have told her numerous times to stop wasting my money!"

"Why, Rufus, what did she buy?" asked Clifford curiously.

"She bought medication for her mother."

"Oh, Rufus, Lydia's mother needs that medication."

"Clifford, I cannot deny the fact that her mother needs medication, but it's my money, it's my bloody money! I go to work! I work hard! She's not my mother! And she goes through her medication like tap water. I reckon she sells the medication on eBay for more money."

"Blimey, Rufus, that is a horrendous accusation to make."

Rufus suffered from a lack of sensitivity and care. He was not liked very much, but he was not bothered by other people until money was involved. "I have always had my suspicions about Lydia's mother," he said, shaking his head and squinting.

"Whatever for?" asked Clifford.

"When her uncle died she was the only person who wasn't crying."

"That doesn't mean anything, Rufus, she probably grieved in her own time."

"Clifford, she was rubbing her hands, smiling gaily and humming the Abba song, 'Money, Money, Money'."

Clifford thought that was slightly odd but said nothing.

Still driving on the way to work, Rufus was still complaining to Clifford. This time it was about the kosher milkman. "Can you believe it, Clifford, the milkman does not deliver kosher milk anymore. That is disgraceful. I cannot have normal milk from such common places such as Tesco or Sainsbury's, that is the poor people's milk."

"What about milk from Iceland? That is the place where I buy mine from."

"Especially not Iceland!" Clifford snapped. "Nothing is kosher in that place."

"That's true," agreed Clifford. "Not even the pork is kosher," said Clifford bluntly, not really thinking about what he just said. Rufus panicked as he was in the presence of someone mentioning a type of food coming from a pig. Rufus did not hesitate to text his local rabbi to ask for repentance for 'my non-Jewish friend'.

Meanwhile, back at the Cockflint household, Lydia was going through an emotional meltdown. Drenched tissues lay all around the patient's chair. Every time Lydia's session was over Christine went around picking up her tissues, and they were so wet that it normally left several damp patches on her cream carpet.

"Oh, Christine, I cannot take it anymore, this feeling of getting older and older by the minute. I no longer feel the vibrant woman that I once was. My body needs a damn good ironing, my mind is always in turmoil and at night I am finding it extremely difficult to fall asleep. Then the irony of it all is that I find it difficult to stay awake during the day. I must look like a gormless corpse."

Christine was finding Lydia challenging to understand as she continuously blew her nose on her tissues. Christine thought to herself that next time she would give her a bathroom towel. "And have you spoken to Rufus about all this?" questioned Christine, simultaneously scribbling down some notes on her clipboard.

"Christine, you must be joking! Me, Lydia Feldman, talk to my husband about my problems?" Lydia rubbed her neck smirking knowing that Rufus would not care. "We don't talk about anything anymore, all he cares about is his professional status. His charm that I fell in love with twenty-nine years ago has gone completely. Financially everything is okay, although the way Rufus talks you would think we live in poverty. Sometimes I do not think we seem like a married couple. At parties he is with his friends at one end of the hall and I am at the other end, bored out of my brains."

"Well, Lydia, this may seem like a personal question, well to be honest it is a personal question, but are you and Rufus intimate?" Christine always found it helpful in her job if she dug deep for answers. This way she knew which pathway to take with her patients.

"Absolutely not, there is no passionate soul in that man. Only the other night I was in bed and Rufus walked in completely and utterly naked. He then walked up to me seductively and I felt like the princess being rescued by the courageous, brave knight from the tall tower. Suddenly he turned, bent down till his hands were touching his feet and said, 'Lydia, love, do you think my haemorrhoids have shrunk'." Lydia then started crying again. Christine felt very sorry for her and secretly wrote down that she must speak to Rufus in her next session with him. "Christine, Rufus even suspects that my mother is robbing us. I buy her medication because she cannot afford to buy regular supplies, and now he is saying that she sells her medication online."

"Really? Oh, Lydia, that's terrible."

"Christine, this is what I am talking about. His brain cooks up all these stupid ideas that are far from reality."

As Christine was writing down some information in her notepad she suddenly realised something. "Lydia, please forgive me for asking such a question but isn't your mother married to one of the richest Jewish men in Great Britain?" Christine prepared herself for the worst reaction.

"Yes," said Lydia calmly, not considering or processing any suspicious thoughts that had been brought to the table.

"Then why are you paying for her medical treatment if she is married to one of the richest Jewish men?" said Christine.

"Mummy doesn't like taking money from my stepfather. She only likes spending Rufus's money." Christine soon realised why Rufus grumbled about his mother in law all the time. "Anyway, Christine, I am here to talk about myself and Rufus, not my mother."

"Yes, of course, Lydia," she said, scribbling more notes on the paper.

"Many husbands would do anything for their wives, but not mine. Once there was this puddle and I was the one who had to carry Rufus over it because he was worried that his new shoes would get ruined."

"Lydia, we all have our strange idiosyncrasies."

"Yes, but this puddle went on for a mile. Then he felt bad and said to me that he should not have allowed me to hold him for that long because of my age!"

The appointment went on longer than the given time but this did not bother Christine as all Lydia's appointments went way over the given time.

Lydia's tears began again.

TWO

Every day when Clifford dropped Rufus off at work he drives home a different route taking a nice steady pace through the countryside. Clifford and Christine were keen walkers and they walked miles through the wild forests and steep hills. It was a haven of relaxation for them to unwind. It did take Clifford approximately eighty minutes to get home but that did not bother him as Christine knew where he was. As he approached some traffic lights a man waved him down to stop. Clifford did so and pulled up alongside him.

"Hi there, sir, what is the problem? Has there been a crash?"

"No, no, sir I just wanted to inform you that this country road will be closed off from tomorrow until next month while there are roadworks going on."

"Ah, thank you for that warning, I'll take the non-pretty route home from tomorrow onwards," said Clifford laughing. He thanked the man again and drove home to Christine. Clifford did begin to notice the potholes in the road, and they looked like the size of mines. "Thank goodness these roads are being seen to," said Clifford driving down the steep narrow hill.

Christine was in the middle of a session with her second patient. It was in fact her neighbour from the other side. She was a very young lady engaged to her strict Catholic fiancée. They were both twenty-two. Sarah's fiancée, Simon, was brought up by strict Catholic parents who lived by the holy bible, and this attitude had rubbed off on him. Sarah, on the other hand, was a Catholic but her parents were not strict about the Catholic upbringing. They reluctantly went to church on a Saturday when Sarah was younger, but they refused to go on a Sunday morning because her parents liked to lay in bed till twelve o'clock. Sarah devoted her life to Simon. She was besotted by him and was counting down the hours until that very moment when she would be standing at the altar with him. Sarah broadcasted her love for Simon and she wanted just two things from him. One, for him to express his love for her emotionally and physically. Two, for him to spend more time with her. Simon worked in an office twelve hours a day, six days a week and then in the evening for two and a half hours he would be down the church conducting some presentation about the Catholic faith. Sarah was another woman who sought Christine's advice and help. "He is not demanding, Christine, sometimes I even wonder if he realises that I am in the house with him. On Sundays, which is his day off, from ten o'clock till one thirty he is at the church, then when he gets home he sits at the kitchen table and completely analyses *The Catholic Commodity* from cover to cover, word by word. He has no time for me. Three hours on a Sunday is not enough time."

Christine did not understand religion. She gave up on being a Catholic when she got cancer and suffered terribly. Clifford was unhappy with Christine's change of mood as he told her that she should thank God that she got better. Christine worried that one day if it returned she might not be so lucky, however, she considered herself lucky to have such a supporting husband like Clifford because if she had a husband like Rufus or Simon she would have found it difficult to cope.

"Simon is afraid to do anything with me, and that's not right. I don't know how to reset his mind. Christine, I guarantee that if I said to Simon that he has to sell me or his bible at a car boot sale I'd be gone in seconds."

"Sarah, you are a beautiful girl" said Christine reassuringly. "Simon loves you and he would not sell you over a bible."

Sarah murmured to herself.

"Sarah, we agreed that if you were unhappy with something I said please say," said Christine feeling guilty.

"Christine, I am not exaggerating when I say these things. I know Simon better than anyone."

"Does Simon know you better than anyone?" asked Christine tapping her pencil against her clipboard.

"Simon says that no one knows him better than God."

Christine found it difficult not to giggle.

"All my friends tell me that Simon is boring and that I could do much better. I hate it when they say that because they never get to see the side of him that I know and love." Sarah continued to speak for another fifteen minutes, then they both heard the front door open and in popped Clifford.

"I'm home, Christine. I'll make some vegetable soup for lunch along with hot rolls to go with it," he said shouting from the bottom of the stairs.

"Sounds lovely," Christine called back.

"That is why, Christine, you are so good at your job," said Sarah.

"What do you mean?" asked Christine curiously.

"You and Clifford have such a happy relationship. I really admire that and you have both been together for twenty-one years."

"Twenty-eight years," corrected Christine.

"Unbelievable," said Sarah, completely shocked at the idea of something lasting for such a long time. "I hope you and Clifford never separate."

"We are a match made in heaven," said Christine, laughing but with a pinch of sarcasm.

"Please don't say heaven," said a shuddering Sarah. "I come here to get away from all that carry on."

When Sarah left Clifford had prepared lunch. He set the table as if they were at a restaurant as that was the way they both liked it. They enjoyed the ambience of eating together. Clifford liked cooking and when he was a teenager he worked at his local Chinese takeaway when one day he asked the head chef if he could teach him how to cook. So every day Clifford would stay and watch the chef cook a meal and Clifford would try and copy. After practising so many times he eventually qualified with the life skills of cooking. Working at the Chinese takeaway was the best thing Clifford could have ever done because it was also the place where he met Christine. Clifford refused to give two *Jeremy Kyle Show* lookalikes their money back because they were unhappy with their food even though they ate it quite happily. The two trolls were women and they called in their fat Indian husbands. They and Clifford got into a scrap, then Christine's parents stepped in and helped Clifford. All this happened without the chef knowing because he was busy making curry sauce in the back. Clifford thanked his unknown future in-laws. The next time her parents went in Christine went with them. They both had an

13

interesting and deep conversation and then their romance blossomed from there.

"Lemonade or freshly squeezed lychees?" asked Clifford, holding a bowl of lychees and a bottle of lemonade in his hands.

"Lychees please, Clifford."

Clifford brought two bowls of soup and two glasses of drinks through on a tray for them both. Clifford's vegetable soup was legendary within the area. At parties he was often asked to make a pot of it, parties such as christenings, weddings, school meetings and for the over sixties club. Clifford was more than happy to do that as he loved making it. The only person who refused to eat it was Rufus. He did worry that Clifford cooked it in dishes that non-kosher food had been prepared in, but no matter how many times Clifford assured Rufus it was not enough. "Burdensome, sex-absent, fault-finding old Jew," Clifford would say repeatedly.

"So, Christine, any improvements with Lydia or Sarah?" asked Clifford being nosey.

"Not really. Simon does not realise that Sarah is there in the house and Rufus is being Rufus towards Lydia." Christine reached out for a delicious hot roll and buttered it.

"That is a shame," said Clifford. "Sarah and Simon should be going down to the local nightclubs. Regarding Rufus and Lydia they are at the prime of their marriage. They should be going to the theatre, going on more holidays, in other words enjoying life."

"Exactly," said Christine agreeing. Clifford and Christine enjoyed every moment of living.

"Oh, but they're Jewish. There is no hope of Rufus spending money," said Clifford, dipping his hot roll into his soup.

"Don't be silly, Clifford." Suddenly they both glared at each other then broke out into a fit of laughter.

Later that day Clifford drove to pick up Rufus from the school where they both worked. Normally he got home between six thirty and seven o'clock. Lydia had prepared dinner, she had cooked roasted figs in honey with bagels, then ginger beer cake for dessert. As both Rufus and Lydia were strict Jews Lydia always cooked traditional food. She did not relish going to other people's houses for dinner as one time Clifford cooked a meal full of pork, then in a panic Clifford remembered about Jewish people not eating pork and told them it was kosher pork hoping they would fall for it. Furthermore, Lydia constantly refused dinner invitations from Sarah and Simon as the last time they met up Rufus and Simon ended up debating viciously on religious backgrounds. However, Lydia and Sarah got on well even though there was thirty-two years between them. Christine, Lydia and Sarah were all great friends despite some of their marital troubles. When Rufus got home he kissed Lydia on the head softly then they sat down to dinner. All was going well until Rufus spoke out of turn.

"Oh my rabbi! Lydia, you're getting more lines on your face then lined paper," said Rufus, as he bit into a bagel.

"Get out of the room, Rufus! Get out right this minute you insensitive, poor excuse of a man!" Lydia picked up a plate and threw it high hitting the wall. Pieces of broken china fell everywhere.

"Lydia, don't be so angry. Oh, bloody fantastic, there is cake stuck against my sweaty back," said Rufus picking off bits of the cake.

"Good, and do not think you'll be sleeping with me tonight, Rufus Feldman, because you're not. Although if you were there I wouldn't notice anyway."

Clifford and Christine listened to the shouting that was happening next door. It was like watching *EastEnders*, *Coronation Street* and *Emmerdale* rolled into one. Clifford flinched twice as he heard two plates smash against the wall.

On the other side Christine saw the invisible Simon arrive home from work. "Oh dear, Clifford, it's going to be argument number two of the evening. If only we had Terry and June as neighbours."

Simon walked in dumping his briefcase by the front door. Sarah walked up to him to give him a warm kiss.

"Hello, darling," said Sarah, stretching out her arms wide to give him a hug.

"Oi, get off, get off, we're not married yet," said Simon doing the sign of the cross.

"Oh, for heaven's sake, Simon, we are allowed to hug. I'm not committing a crime."

Simon could not contain his upset from Sarah's outburst. "Blasphemous, Sarah, blasphemous! You're in a frightfully sinister disposition tonight. Thank the Lord I am going down to the church. It'll give you time to calm down." Simon took off his tie and went upstairs to get changed.

"I am only in a mood because you act like you're forty-five not twenty-two. What about me, Simon, you know, that woman you're engaged to? I had no idea that I would be a single married woman."

"Now you're speaking absolute nonsensical rubbish," said Simon, talking to Sarah from the top of the stairs.

Clifford and Christine sat on the sofa eating popcorn and listening attentively to the rows. "Do you know what I think, Clifford?" said Christine suddenly sitting up with a light flashing in her mind.

"What is that, Christine?" said Clifford with a mouthful of popcorn.

"Lydia and Rufus, Sarah and Simon are missing children from their lives."

"Well, Lydia has more chance of being mugged by Fred Flintstone and Barney Rubble, as for Simon and Sarah they are a bit young, aren't they?"

"There is always adoption for Lydia and Rufus, and all in good time for Sarah and Simon."

As Clifford and Christine sat there listening to more plates smashing and more shouting, Clifford remembered that their children lived in New York and Australia. Suddenly them not being at home hit him hard, particularly that Clifford had not taught for more than half a year. Now he missed his job. Clifford had always strived to help others and he thought it was better to help others from a young age, but he glimpsed over at Christine and knew that for now his duties were dedicated to her. After the arguments calmed down, due to Simon not being in the house and Rufus spending the night at his mother's house, Clifford and Christine went to bed. Then there was a loud knocking on the door.

"Down you go, Christine," said Clifford yawning.

"No way, Clifford, you're the man of the house," said Christine stubbornly.

Clifford had always said that if someone was to break in during the night it would destroy his confidence as that was his biggest fear. "Oh don't be so stereotypical," Clifford replied sharply. He went downstairs putting on his round orange spectacles and opened the door to a frenzied Lydia.

"Oh, Clifford, please let me stay the night, I can hear voices talking in the street, and without a doubt it will be burglars wanting to break into my lovely, rich, expensive, well looked after house full of golden materials..."

"Okay!" Clifford interrupted. "That's fine, Lydia, The spare room... well, you know where the spare room is, you have slept in it often enough." With that Clifford went back to bed as Lydia made herself comfortable in the spare room. She had slept in that room so many times that she had her own wallpaper in there. She turned off her lamp and went to bed. All was quiet. Literally two minutes later after Clifford had dozed off there was another loud knock coming from the front door. Clifford casually walked downstairs, opened the door and said, "Lydia is in the spare room, Sarah, but there is always the other spare room." Sarah went upstairs. Clifford followed close behind. She went into the other spare room and went to bed. Clifford laid in his bed. By this time it was three twenty in the morning, when suddenly he jumped with consternation. "Oh my word, Christine, please don't be dead!" He turned on the light and saw that Lydia was on the bed whispering to Christine. Clifford's hand was on Lydia's arm.

Lydia growled like a guard dog. "What do you mean, 'Christine, please don't be dead!'" snapped Lydia.

"Sorry, Lydia, I have never felt a cold, rough, lizard-like skin in all my life."

"Right, get out of this bed now, Clifford." Lydia angrily pointed to the door and Clifford walked out of the bedroom slamming the door tightly behind him, then realising that he had just been kicked out of his own bed, but he was too tired to argue so he went to bed in the spare room where Lydia was meant to sleep.

THREE

The next morning Clifford found it a little cramped at breakfast so he took two cereal bars in the car with him. As usual he was due to pick up Rufus, however, the argument between Rufus and Lydia meant that Clifford had to drive through town to get him as his mother lived on the other side of town. During the mornings the traffic was horrendous and very stressful for any driver and Clifford thought that it was a job he could have done without. Clifford said goodbye to the ladies at breakfast but they were too busy speaking to even acknowledge that he had gone.

Eventually Clifford finally made it to Rufus's parents and parked outside the gates. He was in no mood to be kept waiting so Clifford blasted the car horn. Rufus ran out thinking there was an emergency.

"What's the problem, Clifford, what is the hurry?" said Rufus panting like an obese child running after the ice-cream van.

"Your wife kicked me out of my own bed last night. You must stop walking out on each other every time you have a row."

"But, Clifford, she kicked *me* out, plus she threw out some harsh insults, and, let me tell you, it hurt more than having a brick thrown at you." Rufus turned his head away and folded his arms. He looked like an overgrown toddler.

"No! Not insults, Rufus, Lydia told you some home truths."

"Don't be stupid, Clifford."

"No, no, I am not being stupid, Rufus. You are a sour, bitter person."

"Clifford!" said a shocked and outraged Rufus. "I am a loving person who showers my wife with love and compassion."

Clifford rolled his eyes in disbelief. "You are talking a load of rubbish! Loving? Showers wife with love? Compassion? Ha!" said Clifford sarcastically, finding it difficult to take Rufus's words seriously.

"Why are you saying it like that?" enquired Rufus now totally bemused.

"You really don't have a clue, do you?" said Clifford.

"Clifford, this is unlike you."

"Why?" asked Clifford.

"You are being very temperamental this morning. We should have ordered two coffees from the drive-through."

"What! Something else I would have had to pay for," Clifford snapped.

"Excuse me, Clifford, I would have got the coffees. Are you insinuating that I am tight with money?"

"So what you're telling me is that you would have happily bought the coffees?"

"Of course I would have!" Rufus shouted. "As long as we ordered the small cups, preferably just one small cup, one small cup with two straws, and maybe that small cup would only be filled halfway."

"Rufus, please stop talking," said Clifford, digging his fingers into the steering wheel.

"Clifford, I am not spending more than eight pence on one cup of coffee," said Rufus bluntly.

"Okay, let's change the subject," said Clifford, feeling fed up with his neighbour.

"But you're the one who mentioned coffee," said Rufus.

"Sorry, now I realise that I should not mention anything about buying a coffee in the morning."

"Please don't let me stop you from talking about coffee..."

"Just drop it, Rufus! Okay!" said Clifford interrupting.

Stubbornly Rufus did not say anything until Clifford dropped him off at school. "Goodbye, Clifford, see you later."

"Maybe," said Clifford, and drove off.

Rufus had never seen Clifford that annoyed before, but he was suddenly distracted when he saw two students smoking inside the school grounds. "Oi! I am going to confiscate those cigarettes. Obviously you're not Jewish students otherwise you would not be smoking and especially at your age."

"Shut it, old man," said one disrespectful student.

"How dare you! Right, to the headmaster's office at once."

"Erm, Mr Feldman, you are the headmaster."

"Right, that's it! Detention for a month. This is not the first time I've caught you. Last time I caught you both smoking on the field."

"But, sir, that was a year ago."

"Excuse me, lad, do not answer me back! To the office and step on it!" Rufus ran a tight ship at his school although he did miss Clifford being there. The students respected Clifford and the English teacher who took over temporarily was not respected at all. In fact Rufus was always speaking to irritated parents about her teaching methods. Clifford's cover was a Miss Nice although ironically she was a monster. Students and Rufus alike could not wait for Clifford to return.

On his way home Clifford felt highly ratty. Both his neighbours were beginning to annoy him, but a drive through the countryside would distract him. However, the drive distracted him too much as he went off into a daydream. The car was speeding along the road when Clifford failed to see what was in front of him. A road sign stood in the middle of the road telling drivers that the road up ahead was closed, but Clifford missed this sign. There were no workers about, they had all gone to get some lunch, but it was too late for Clifford. The car smashed through the warning sign with an almighty crash and slid off the road. The four wheels took off from the ground and sent the car rolling down a steep hill heading for the forest. Clifford tried desperately to bring the car to a halt but it was completely out of control. He was being thrown backwards and forwards, to and fro and his glasses had fallen from his face. In no time the car had entered the forest and was approaching a bridge that had been built thousands of years ago. The car got halfway across but the bridge could not take the weight and finally gave way. Wreckage of the bridge and the car plunged into the water below. The rapids dragged the car along the watery and muddy ravine which was getting tighter and tighter and suddenly the car became wedged in between some rocks. Clifford tried to find his spectacles and at the same time he peeped over the top of the car to see if he could make his getaway. He found his spectacles but the force of the water smashed the car through the tight rocks. The car once again was being carried along by the water. The inside had been scratched, damaged and practically destroyed and the water poured through the ceiling. Clifford managed to stick his head out from the top of the car only to notice that he was nearing a small waterfall. He got ready to make a jump for it. The car plunged down the waterfall but at the same time Clifford jumped from the roof and together the car and Clifford plunged into the water below and the power of the waves pushed him to the side of the muddy embankment. His head ended up in a deep patch of mud. He pulled his head out and laid there to recover.

FOUR

"Last night we had a massive argument," said Sarah, gazing up at the ceiling. Arguments depressed Sarah. She had never been able to get on with the day knowing that an argument had not been resolved.

"Really? That surprises me because myself and Clifford did not hear a thing," Christine lied to avoid upsetting her.

"That's a relief. I did wonder last night just before I went to bed if you and Clifford heard us. I was not entirely sure whether or not the walls were thin."

Christine changed the conversation and moved to another topic. "So, this argument, was that the reason you stayed last night? Did you feel the need to get out of that environment? Did you feel unsafe? Unloved? Unprotected?"

"Yes, yes, no, yes, yes. I would never feel scared of Simon, he is a very kind person in that respect. However, it's his feelings towards me. I am not sure if I can live with his obsessiveness and dedication to his religion. I certainly will never change him, his principles are too high."

"He does not necessarily have to change his ways, he just needs to schedule more time for you."

"Miracles do not happen very often," said Sarah.

"Oh, Sarah, that is not the right attitude to take. I will help you, then you and Simon should hopefully be able to work something out."

"Well, I really hope we can sort something out. Last night was just terrible."

"Take last night as experience and now work from it and move forward," said Christine trying to reassure Sarah. Christine put her hand into a plastic bag and pulled out a book. "Sarah, I bought this book yesterday and I thought it might interest you." Christine handed Sarah the book and she studied the front cover.

She read the title aloud: *"Books for Dummies: How to Understand Obsessive Likings and all the Bollocks That Comes With*

It." Sarah nodded happily. "Thank you, Christine. I will read this from cover to cover."

A little while later Sarah's session had come to an end. When she left Christine sat at her desk writing up Sarah's notes. When she saw her appointment book she contemplated booking a slot for Simon. "Good morning, neighbour," said Lydia unexpectedly.

"Why are you saying good morning? You were here this morning," Christine laughed.

"While you were busy up here doing things, I noticed Sarah going home. Was she up here with you?" asked Lydia quizzically.

"Oh, Sarah was up here…" Christine quickly stopped herself. She nearly broke the code of confidentiality. "Nothing, Sarah just asked me if I needed a pint of milk."

Lydia was not even listening to her. She had the terrible habit of not listening to other people when she was dying to tell people her news. "I went home, and obviously Rufus did not come home this morning. The house was cold, so he must have stayed with his miserable, boring and old parents."

"Do you want to talk about Rufus?" asked Christine, preparing herself for another session.

"No thank you, Christine," said Lydia, then Christine put everything away. Then Lydia changed her mind and sat on the chair. Christine rolled her eyes.

"During the night I had this tremendous brainwave. I thought to myself the reason I feel old, unloved and tired is because I act like an old lady and I am not strict enough with Rufus. I need to put my foot down and whip that little man into shape."

"Do you think that would help?" asked Christine scribbling away on her notes.

"Oh, absolutely!" said Lydia, then she remembered something else she wanted to tell Christine. "Do you know, two weeks ago we went to the Jewish bingo night. Rufus hates Jewish bingo night with a passion because he has to spend money. He's an idiot. During the game Rufus was winning nothing, but I wasn't even winning but then it doesn't bother me as it is all part of the game. However, on the last page Rufus needed just one more number to win three thousand pounds. At this point he was shaking as he was waiting for number eighteen to be called. The bingo caller shouted 'eight, forty-eight, fifty-eight', but he had not called eighteen. Rufus was swearing under his breath, 'Come on, you bastard, call number eighteen, you bastard, just call it, I never win anything worthwhile, you complete and utter bastard'. Honestly, Christine, his language was appalling," said Lydia. "Then the bingo caller suffered a heart attack. He just fell forward and the game came to a halt. Rufus went mental. As the paramedics were carrying the bingo caller out on a stretcher Rufus followed him out calling him a selfish bastard." Lydia laid back and said nothing. She just stared into space for a moment. Then she softly said, "Listen, Christine, I don't suppose you fancy a trip into town? I am in the mood to start all over again. I need new clothes."

"What about Rufus?" Christine said worryingly, as she knew the outcome would be negative if Rufus found out she had spent money.

"Forget Rufus. Let's go!"

Christine did love shopping. Lydia rushed home to quickly get her belongings and the car. Christine left a note for Clifford telling him that she would be back in the evening some time.

The car was already out when Christine locked up the house. She got into the passenger's seat with all her bags.

"Were you leaving a note for Clifford?" asked Lydia pulling off.

"I thought I had better just in case he gets home soon. He should be home in about fifteen minutes. Either that or he does a runner," Christine joked, unaware of the danger that Clifford was in.

FIVE

In the middle of nowhere at the bottom of a waterfall, Clifford stood naked washing himself and his clothes. The mud had seeped right through onto his body and was irritating his skin. He repeatedly scratched himself but found it impossible to ignore the problem, therefore he stripped naked and washed himself in the water. Clifford felt dazed and bewildered, he had never experienced such a dramatic crash in his life. This is a new one for the book, he thought. Last time Clifford had felt this dizzy he was on his stag do when someone in the club spiked his drink. Consequently he ended up bouncing off the walls, and when he awoke the next morning he swore that he would never drink again or allow someone to buy him a drink of any kind. He hung his clothes over a tree branch hoping the wind would dry them. Clifford sat contemplating on how he was going to escape and get home before Christine started worrying. He was not bothered how Rufus got home, that did not particularly worry him, and he cheered up a little because he was picturing Rufus having to get the bus home with all the other workers meaning that he would have to mix with the working classes.

As time was ticking Clifford felt to see if his clothes were dry. They were still wet. Clifford stood up to look what was around him. All was quiet.

Then, all of a sudden, a gust of wind caught his clothes. Clifford tried to grab them but the wind blew them into the air and through the forest. Clifford was horrified. He was not wearing a stitch of clothing but was not too worried at being stark naked in the middle of a forest because no one would see him. Clifford frantically ran after his clothes with all his saggy bits waving in the air. They landed in a field in long, wet grass. He ran up to them and picked up his trousers when, and if by magic, a man appeared in front of him and grabbed him. Clifford staggered back aghast. The strange man was not wearing any clothes either.

"Hello, sir," said the stranger, "I see you have come to join us."

Clifford now thought that he was positively losing it. He had just had a major car crash, had his clothes blown away in a wind frenzy, and now all of a sudden he is speaking to a naked man. Clifford reluctantly spoke back to him. "Join? Join who?" he said gobsmacked.

"Us nudists," the man said stepping back and indicating his hand towards a bunch of nudists walking around the field completely naked. Men and women were talking to each other as if what they were doing was normal. "Come on, join us, friend, we do not believe in wearing clothes and let everything hang loose. An artist will be along in a minute to paint an image of us."

Clifford felt freaked out. He would never want anyone to know about this and have a picture painted of himself with a load of naked people, and he knew if anyone heard about this they would not believe him. He felt that if there was evidence of him standing with a group of nudists the evidence would definitely come back to haunt him.

"If it's all the same with you, I would like to make a move please, my wife might be wondering where I've got to."

"Friend, we do not worry here, everything is calm." The sound of the nudist's voice was frightening, it almost sounded threatening.

"Well I am not," Clifford answered back with confidence. "I really need to go."

"Your wife could join us too."

"No, no, that is out of the question." Clifford started to walk away, then he began to walk faster and faster as he realised that the man was beginning to run after him.

Suddenly the man blew his whistle and shouted, "Attention all nudists! Attention all nudists! This man wants to escape and not join our society. Let's stop him!"

Clifford anticipated being chased by hundreds of naked people in the middle of a field. He was running at the pace of a demented, exhausted surgeon escaping from Katie Price. The nudists were catching up with Clifford, and he was panting remembering that he was not the teenager he used to be. The hundreds of feet that were stamping on the ground made the entire field shake. Birds flew from their nests and wild animals ran back to their habitats. Even the wolves hid. Clifford put all his energy and effort into this tenacious run for life. His feet slid in the wet grass, and as he was running he held on to his clothes for dear life. As he continued to run he got closer and closer towards the forest until he was actually in the forest. Clifford looked behind him and could see the nudists were still after him. "Blimey, these freaks do not give up." As he was running through the forest he slipped down a muddy hill and rolled down it, but still managed to hold on to his clothes. His sore body crashed into a tree, and nearby was a hole so he hid there for a while. Luckily the nudists had disappeared. Clifford looked at himself. His back was bleeding, his stomach had open wounds and his hands were in a right state. It was inevitable that he needed medical attention. Clifford considered himself lucky that his spectacles were not broken then he looked up to see the sun in between the tree branches when a bird defecated on his left lens.

"Brilliant, that's just wonderful." He delicately took his spectacles off trying to dodge the bird faeces and cleaned them on some dead leaves. "Now, what next?" He looked at his surroundings. "I need help." Clifford, with effort, cleaned his spectacles. He looked at his reflection in the lenses and he felt that he looked utterly metamorphosed. He was flabbergasted that it was really his reflection. "Oh no, what has happened to me? I hope I survive. What's Bear Grylls' number?" he said to himself.

Christine and Lydia were still out shopping. Lydia had a bad tendency to spend lots of money on little things. Christine bought materials that she needed. Lydia bought things to make herself feel better. Lydia was buying young clothes to make her feel young, therefore she was purchasing loads of clothes from Topshop. Teenage girls were staring at her closely feeling embarrassed that an older lady was trying on clothes for an eighteen year old. One of the girls took up the courage to ask her what she was doing. "Excuse, miss, but I really admire you for buying clothes in here."

Lydia was not in the slightest taken aback that someone actually spoke to her. She felt she was being a role model representing the older types. "Thank you, love, I will take that as a compliment."

"Please do, I was not being in the least sarcastic. I really mean it," said the girl reassuringly.

Lydia beamed happily at the fact that younger girls looked up to her because she refused to act old just because she was in the process of going through the menopause. Christine was quite surprised by the amount of attention people were showing Lydia as attention was something that Lydia failed to get. Christine felt that this could be her cure. If Rufus was not going to give her the attention then she could find it from other people. The public watched her in the shop as she went up to the jewellery section and pulled a ridiculous number of necklaces, gold chains, golden rings and bracelets off the wall and wore them there and then in the shop. The girls were tweeting pictures of her and they were being retweeted instantly. Christine sat and watched closely at the impressed public. Lydia was loving every moment of this but after a while she decided to call it a day. In the car Lydia spoke endlessly about how delighted she was at the prospect of being worshipped by young people.

"Oh, Christine, what a day! Did you hear those girls? They worshipped me, I feel completely revitalised."

"Lucky you, at least you and Rufus will have something to talk about."

"You must be joking. Christine, today was a real eye-opener for me. I am going to kick Rufus into touch, and if he does not improve his ways I will leave him for good." Lydia was being serious. She now knew what she wanted and there was no going back.

"Lydia, that's a bit harsh you know. You cannot change someone within a matter of seconds." Christine did enjoy being in Lydia's company but there was a lot of elements about her that Christine disagreed with.

"Tough I'm afraid, Christine! If he refuses to change his ways then he can go and whistle." Christine felt that there was nothing she could do except nod and smile.

"Christine, because I am in such a good mood why don't you come over now and I'll cook us some dinner. I will text Sarah to invite her as well."

"Sounds good," said Christine happily. "I had better tell Clifford I will only be at yours."

"Surely he would see the car. Besides, Christine, the man is in his fifties, surely he can look after himself." Christine hated not telling Clifford where she would be. It was not the fact that Clifford did not trust her, far from it, but she still preferred to say where she was. Clifford always told her where he was, it was just a thing that they had always done.

"Blimey, Lydia, and I thought I was the psychiatrist," laughed Christine jokingly.

As they parked up they saw Sarah and Simon talking in the street. They were hugging each other, then Simon got into a taxi with a suitcase, then the taxi left. Sarah stood there looking glum. Lydia waved her over. Christine had to help Lydia carry her bags into the house.

"Someone has been spending," said Sarah sarcastically.

"Oh, Sarah, I have had a magnificent day," Lydia said loudly.

"Where has Simon gone?" asked a concerned Christine.

"He has gone away for four days to a Catholic convention in York." Sarah's tone was monotonously low. She craved her boyfriend's attention but she knew it was never going to happen.

"I wish Rufus would go on a Jewish convention for days on end. Lucky you, Sarah."

Christine noticed that Clifford's car was not in the driveway, and as the ladies went inside Rufus was absent from the house even though he was due home about an hour ago. Christine assumed that Clifford and Rufus went somewhere so she just ignored any negative thoughts that entered her head.

Rufus stood at the school gates now waiting impatiently for Clifford. He had been standing there for an hour and the clouds were growing darker and darker. Rufus placed his bags and box next to him as it was too heavy for him to hold. He could not go back and wait in his office because the caretaker had locked up the building. "Come on, Clifford, come on, Clifford," he said angrily under his breath. Every car that approached the corner a ray of hope lighted up inside Rufus, but then every car that built his hopes up drove past. His watch grew nearer to seven o'clock then he remembered that Clifford was showing his vengeful side. He picked up all his bags and box and walked hesitantly to the bus stop, a form of travel he thought he would never have to ride. Luckily he had to wait only ten minutes for the bus. As it arrived Rufus could see a lot of people on it, some standing up, the rest sitting down.

As the bus stopped the smell of the fumes nearly knocked him out. When the doors slid opened a cockney woman spoke to him. "Where are you going?" she said showing her toothless smile.

"Castle Avenue," replied Rufus. He could not understand why she would not pay a dental surgeon to have her teeth sorted. As she gave him a ticket he did not want to hold it as he feared he would pick up germs. I am going to kill Clifford for making me go through this nightmare, thought Rufus. Rufus looked straight towards the seats and sat next to a man who he thought looked fine, but as the bus started moving the man felt uncomfortable so he began to fidget. Rufus thought he was going to die, the stench of body odour filled the air and smelled nauseatingly bad. Rufus could not get his head around the fact that a person would leave his home smelling like that. The bus came to its first stop and luckily the man next to Rufus got off. He was delighted and gave a little spray of deodorant which he carried around in his pocket. Another man came and sat in the chair. As he sat there Rufus said nothing to him, and the man was unhappy about that as he liked to be noticed.

"I've had back pain for as long as I care to remember," said the old man making constipated-looking faces.

"That is a shame," said Rufus unconvincingly, because he did not care. "I wouldn't know about pain, I'm Jewish."

"Back in 1948 I was walking along the street when a man started fighting with me. Well, I was not going to take that so I hit him back. It was a pretty damn hard hit too as I knocked him out. The next day he saw me and crossed the road heading in my direction. I thought, Oh oh, here we go again. I was ready to hit him but he shook my hand and said, 'Hello, sir, weren't you the one who hit me yesterday'? Yes, I said, and afterwards we were great friends."

Rufus thought to himself, What the hell was the point in that story? "What stop are you getting off," asked Rufus, hoping that he was going to say the next stop, but the old man was not listening, he was too busy waiting to share his next anecdote.

"In 1953 I bought this shirt and when I got home I saw there was this massive great rip right through the middle of it. So I went back to the shop and I raised hell. I told the sales assistant that I was not happy with the quality of the shirt and then her boss came out. Well, it was only my former boss from my first job. He came and shook my hand, so I told him about my shirt and he said, 'Seymour, because it's you, you can have your money back and a free shirt'. Now if that had been anyone else they would not have got that treatment. He actually did that for me."

Rufus sat there thinking, Why are you telling me this rubbish? Someone please rescue me!

SIX

Clifford walked slowly through the forest. He had not seen a naked body for miles and that was how he wanted it. The water had somehow managed to shrink his clothes slightly and his trousers looked like shorts, and he could not do all his buttons up on his shirt. During the accident he had lost his shoes so he had to walk about barefoot. His feet were in a sorry state by the sticks and stones that stuck in the soles. Clifford walked with an uncomfortable limp; as the hours passed he felt like he had walked miles but seemed to be getting nowhere. The surrounding trees made Clifford feel trapped, and he could not believe how he had allowed himself to get into this state in the first place. If only he had not allowed Rufus to annoy him. Clifford had always been patient and he regretted being pompous and arrogant towards Rufus. Crack! went another branch sticking into the sole of his foot. "Ouch!" yelled Clifford, "that one was painful." As he limped down the pathway he found an old abandoned bicycle lying there in a ditch. He thought that his luck was changing. Happily he slowly climbed down into the ditch and pulled the bicycle out. He cleared all the branches and the remains of the long dangly roots around the tyres. Clifford gently sat on the saddle hoping the bicycle would not collapse and when he cycled slowly backwards and forwards all was fine. Clifford cycled through the forest and his feet were now not as painfully sore as they had been. It was a bumpy ride as he and the bicycle bobbed up and down, and then his spectacles slipped down his face. The bicycle then hit a rock and Clifford was tossed into the air landing on the ground with the bicycle landing on top of him. Clifford was not defeated, he had made it this far and there was no going back. He picked up the bicycle once more and continued on his way.

"And then in 1967 I committed murder. Someone was being disrespectful, therefore I hit him so hard that he fell unconscious and died later in hospital due to severe head injuries, but I knew the judge very well. Oh, we were great friends, we met once when we were standing in a queue and he could see that I needed help, so he carried everything for me. So anyway, at the courts he said, 'Well, Seymour, because we are great friends and I know you I'll just give you a warning'." Rufus was drifting in and out of sleep due to the boredom of listening to Seymour's stories. "There was this man who mugged me for fifty pence and because the judge hated him and really, really, really liked me that mugger faced a prison sentence."

Rufus woke up. "My rabbi, he is still talking, why is he still talking?"

Seymour was well known and people did everything in their power to avoid him. If people saw him approaching they would either walk in the opposite direction or pretend that they were talking on their mobile phones and were in a hurry. The bus pulled up at the bus stop, three stops from where Rufus was due to get off. "Sorry to interrupt your great never-ending story, but my bus stop is not far," Rufus lied trying not to appear rude but just wanting him to stop talking.

"No problem, sir," said Seymour. Suddenly the bus made a terrific noise and came to a stop. Then the bus driver got off.

"Where is he going?" asked Rufus to Seymour.

"Oh the bleeding bus has broken down again."

"Oh, please no! Anything but the bus breaking down," said Rufus, who was losing the will to live. "I am not waiting for another bus, I'll walk home the rest of the way." Rufus stood up, gathered all his belongings, then, zipping up his coat, he picked up his work materials and was about to head off. "I suppose you'll be waiting for the next bus?" Rufus asked Seymour.

"No, I have to walk home now in the opposite direction because my stop was three miles back," replied Seymour.

"Why didn't you get off then?" asked Rufus confused.

"Because I thought you were enjoying my stories so much that I thought I would stay on the bus and finish them off."

Rufus stared in blank amazement. "Enjoying? What are you talking about?" but he said that to himself. He picked up all his bags, jumped off the bus and walked home in frustration. Unfortunately for Rufus the heavens opened, then he started to run until all the papers blew out of his bag. Rufus ran around like a headless chicken trying to find them all in the pouring rain.

Clifford had taken shelter under a tree until the rain had calmed down. As the rain seemed to be coming to an end he stood up and enjoyed a long stretch and walked off to urinate in the bushes when unexpectedly a strong lightning flash struck a tree. The tree toppled over landing on Clifford's bicycle crushing it into pieces. "Oh come on!" shouted Clifford spraying a squirrel with his urine because he had let go.

Meanwhile, the ladies had finished eating a Jewish meal cooked by Lydia. She loved traditional cooking, and Christine and Sarah loved it when they got an invitation to dinner. Lydia was proud of her talents when it came to cooking and her mother had worked in a Jewish restaurant for many years. Every Sunday afternoon when Lydia used to get back from the synagogue her mother would show her how to cook. Eventually Lydia's cooking skills became so well known that anyone who was invited to dinner never turned the invitation down due to their love of Lydia's cooking. However, she was also a fan of Christine's cooking, and Christine often organised evening meals for her neighbours who loved socialising and eating together.

"Lydia, that was delicious," Christine thanked her wiping her mouth with a napkin.

"I have to agree with Christine," said Sarah, "That really was a dinner."

"Thank you, ladies," replied Lydia. "Fear not, there will be plenty more meals like it in the future." She stood up removing the plates from the ladies when Rufus came in huffing and puffing with a load of damaged paper on his person and a soaking wet suit. His raincoat, unfortunately, had failed to keep his clothes dry.

"Rufus, what's happened to you?" asked Lydia as she put the plates back onto the table in fear of dropping them.

"Your husband, Christine, that's who! He was angry with me this morning and cannot get over it. He failed to pick me up this evening and left me to get on a smelly bus. Then I had to sit next to a bullshitting old prick and then the blessed bus broke bloody down!"

"Rufus, don't swear!" screeched Lydia.

Butterflies were swimming about in Christine's stomach. She felt ill all of a sudden as she knew that Clifford would not have held grudges and that he should have been home by now. "Hang on a minute, Rufus, I have not seen Clifford all day. Come to think of it the car has not been parked in the driveway. He must have gone somewhere."

"He'll be going somewhere when I get my hands on him."

"Oh, Rufus, hush your violent tongue!" shouted Lydia again.

Lydia's shopping bags were strewn across the carpet in front of Rufus. She prepared herself expecting the worst. If there was one thing that made Rufus explode it was when Lydia had spent his money unwisely. Sarah also stood there in anticipation as she too knew what Rufus was like when it came to money.

"No, Lydia, please don't tell me you've spent a load of my money, my well earned money on clothes for you."

Lydia was fed up with her husband for ever shouting at her and keeping her trapped in the house. A flashback occurred and she reflected at all the years Rufus had been upsetting and hurtful towards her. "Yes, Rufus, I spent money, and lots of it!"

"You stupid cow!" Rufus ran towards the computer to check his bank balance. "You've spent one thousand four hundred pounds on clothes, food and other accessories." Rufus looked at the bags. "You've bought clothes from Topshop but you're far too old now, Lydia. What were you thinking? Age concern is more your line."

"You slimy piece of rubbish! I might even spend more tomorrow."

"Don't you dare, otherwise I will cancel all the credit cards and you will never see them again!" Just as the argument was about to escalate, Sarah got their attention by banging her hand against the table. "What!" the couple shouted in unison.

"While you two selfish people have been arguing about flipping money, Christine has gone home worried why Clifford is not home yet. Don't you both realise that at this precise moment in time Clifford could be in serious trouble?"

That night Christine was being interviewed by the local community police, and she gave them a description of Clifford plus a picture for identification.

"Thank you, madam, I know it's easy enough for me to say this but please do not worry, we are dealing with this."

"Brilliant, thank you for your help." Christine showed the policemen out then, shutting the door behind them, she felt emotional and riddled with guilt. She knew there would be no point in worrying as she knew that the policemen were at work. She contemplated whether or not to go out and look for Clifford herself, however, the policemen did order her to stay at home at all times just in case he shows up. As difficult as it was for her she stayed put and tried to get on with her chores. Christine secretly rung Rufus checking that he would still turn up for his appointment in the morning, and he agreed he would be there.

SEVEN

Clifford attempted to build a small shelter for himself with sticks so he could sleep underneath it but the wind kept blowing it down. After the sixth attempt he gave up and in the end he started a fire to keep himself warm. He thought although he did not have shelter then at least he could get some warmth. He sat on the ground leaning up against a tree when he realised his watch was missing. He was adamant that Christine would have known that he was lost. Rufus would know that he was lost too and Clifford panicked thinking that Christine had informed the police of his disappearance. He had never been missing for this long before, plus he was in the middle of the forest with no sense of time and no materials on him. It was literally him and the rags on his back. Clifford held his hand out in front of his face. The darkness of the night was pitch black and his hand seemed invisible. The moon was shining like a bright torch but the light was not strong enough for Clifford to see his hand. The pounding of his heart seemed extremely loud and he felt weak which was due to how terrified he felt. A forceful wind blew leaves and tree branches all over the place, and the tree branches were breaking off and flying through the air. Clifford was shielding his eyes with his arm as the branches were hitting his face, but the wind was calming down and Clifford's paranoid thoughts were decreasing. The fire illuminated the surroundings of the forest and eventually Clifford drifted into a deep and restful sleep.

The next morning the smoke still wafted in the air but the fire had fizzled out during the night. Clifford opened one eye, then the other, looked around him, then froze in horror. All around the forest laid hundreds of tired wolves. From Clifford's knowledge he knew that they were howling wolves but they were wolves none the less. He was petrified, and he knew he had to escape now and fast. Slowly and steadily Clifford stood up, not moving quickly. He was shaking as he walked over the sleeping wolves. They blocked off the entire footpath. Clifford knew he was skin and bones but the use of his bones would have been a treat for them. As Clifford tried to make his great escape he saw in the distance a group of lumberjacks ready to chop down some trees. The first lumberjack pulled a cord to start a chainsaw. It made such a racket that every single wolf woke from their sleep infuriated that someone or something had disturbed them. Clifford felt the awkwardness of being stared at and he was astonished that animals could make him feel like this. He moved slowly to the right, the wolves in unison moved their heads to the right as well. The wolves did not budge until, "TIMBER!" bellowed the main lumberjack. A tree collapsed to the ground, and when it landed it felt like the entire forest shook.

The wolves took off and ran after Clifford. Hundreds of chafed, bloodthirsty wolves competed with each other to see who could trap Clifford first, rip him up and eat him for breakfast. Frightened, Clifford wished that the nudists were tormenting him now rather than hungry wolves. He was finding it difficult to hurdle over fallen dead trees and run through deep puddles, and it was a miracle that the wolves did not catch up with him. One wolf, however, managed to outrun him and he bit Clifford's leg. "Ouch! You vicious bastard," and he kicked the wolf off him, breaking his jaw in two different places. In the distance was a rope tied to a branch high up in a tree. Clifford with all his strength jumped up high, grabbing onto the rope hoping that it would not snap off, and climbed up with terrific energy. Clifford sat on the tree branch while down below the wolves crowded around the tree waiting for him to come down. He realised that at some point he would have to come down but would not be able to escape the wolves. Clifford needed a miracle and he needed it now.

Christine walked around the area looking for her missing husband, and as Clifford had the car she did not have any form of transport. She had checked the phone answering machine which had no message on it. Christine could hear the common sound of Rufus and Lydia exchanging insults and cursing each other. What with Clifford being missing for several hours and her two best friends upset by their male role models in their lives, Christine suddenly felt a burst of energy explode inside her. She realised that she needed to put her foot down which would hopefully take her mind off

Clifford's search. She opened the front door calling Rufus's name and waving her arm then pointing at her watch indicating to him that their session was about to start.

"Now, Rufus, I hope you do not think that I am going to have a soft attitude towards you because the way you speak to Lydia, your wife of nearly thirty years, is absolutely disgusting."

"Christine, where did that outburst come from?" Rufus was a person used to doing things his own way and never listened to anyone else. Christine knew the way his mind worked and even though Clifford was still missing she was determined to make Rufus realise how he made Lydia feel.

"It's not an outburst, Rufus, it's the damned truth. Lydia is going through a sensitive patch in her life and you calling her old does not exactly help."

"But she is old." Rufus has this unbelievably blunt attitude, and his insufferable mannerisms have got worse as he has got older. He was bullied about his accident and eventually he learnt to like himself because others did not.

"Fifty-four is not old, Rufus! You must be old then!" Christine knew what specific tone to take with Rufus to push his buttons.

"Do you mind, Christine! I am not old, I am in the prime of my years."

"But you're the same age as Lydia!" said Christine getting quite distressed.

"Yes but fifty-four is old for a woman, women look worse when they get older, whereas men look better."

Christine was used to all sorts of answers from her patients and could understand why Lydia felt emotional all the time. "Rufus, has anyone ever told you that you speak the biggest load of rubbish I have ever heard. You are the most truculent person that has ever graced this planet. All men look better as they get older? Do you know how arrogant that sounds?"

"No offence, Christine, but you would say that."

"Okay, now I am going to say something that may come across as personal. I reckon you are the way you are because you cannot get over your accident when you were a child."

Rufus leapt off the patient's chair and then, falling to the floor, started kicking and screaming like a toddler who had been denied an ice-cream. Then he stopped, realising that his moment was over, and sat back on the chair panting for breath. "You have no right bring that up, Christine. You are supposed to be helping me during these sessions, not making me feel worse."

"When are you going to accept the problem?"

"There is no problem," said Rufus, raising his voice.

"You have all these emotional problems, but you cannot express yourself so you take all your anger out on Lydia, the person who has stayed with you all this time. What are you so embarrassed about, is it the fact that you cannot and never have successfully satisfied her physically?"

Both Rufus's cheeks went bright red. "Please, Christine, this is an insane conversation."

"If Lydia left tomorrow would you be upset? Now think about it, would you be upset?"

Rufus sat up and glimpsed out of the window. He was astonished at the fact that someone had opened something in himself that he thought no one could ever do. "After the accident I thought I would never have the confidence to make love to a woman for as long as I lived. It was inevitable that I was going to marry a Jewish lady, and a Jewish lady only, but everyone I dated always came out with the same punchline: 'Blimey, I knew that Jewish males have to be circumcised but I did not realise they took that much off'."

Christine's lips twitched and both her cheeks swelled up. She was dying to laugh but was trying her best not to. "Oh, that is..." she stopped in her tracks trying to hold the laughter in. "That's, that's..."

"Oh, for rabbi's sake, laugh, Christine, go on, laugh. I can tell that you want too. Damnation! You're just like Clifford, he laughed when I told him about this. Now I know what attracted you to each other, your appalling sense of humour."

Christine wiped her eyes with a tissue. She felt awful for laughing but she could not stop. A few minutes later she calmed down and asked Rufus to continue.

"Back in 1979 I was at my cousin's bar mitzvah and my auntie was best friends with Lydia's mother and she brought Lydia along with her. We were both twenty, unmarried and both had little experience of a serious relationship. The mothers were all talking at the table, then when the party got going they all went for a dance leaving me and Lydia together. It was not intentional for us to get together, the mothers did not plan to leave us together on purpose, but after ten minutes we decided to introduce ourselves to each other. To my surprise we got on brilliantly, we both came from a strict Jewish upbringing so it was sex after marriage of course. What with my accident our wedding night did not exactly go off with a bang, but our relationship blossomed into something wonderful that night. However, I feel that when we both hit fifty Lydia and I grew bored of each other."

"No way, Rufus, Lydia loves you, however, the way you act towards her does not work for me. You need to show her much more love, support, understanding and appreciation."

"Fine! I take on board what you say, but I can't say I agree with everything you say."

"Thank you, Rufus." Christine gave him a warm hug and sent him on his way. When she left she rang the police to see how the search operation was coming along.

"I am leaving you, Rufus!" said Lydia, not greeting him with the warmest of welcomes as he entered their bedroom. "I am sick to death of you putting me down. I am leaving and I will not be returning. I am loving the smell of divorce at this particular moment."

"But, Lydia, I am genuinely sorry." Lydia was too angry to take in anything that Rufus was saying to her. She pushed Rufus over, knocking her suitcase into his shin, and he collapsed to the floor in pain. She grabbed her keys and ran for the car. Rufus crawled down the stairs calling out her name. He was desperate for her forgiveness. "Lydia, please wait!"

Lydia stopped at the front door. She knew that later in the day she would feel guilty, but right now she did not care what she said.

"I am going right this minute, you rat. That's it then, twenty-nine years down the drain."

"Lydia!" shouted Rufus. Lydia drove off at the speed of Lewis Hamilton in a grand prix.

Rufus ran back into the house and rang Christine. "Sorry, Christine, I made a mistake."

Lydia drove round the block then discreetly parked her car in Clifford's garage, so that Rufus thought she had gone somewhere far away.

"That man is infuriating," grunted Lydia.

"Honestly, Lydia, I really believed Rufus was trying to make an effort."

"Well it was a pointless effort. He can sit in the house and shrivel for all I care."

"Those are just words you are saying now, Lydia. Now come on, you need to understand that some men fail to communicate with the opposite sex."

"I am hardly a stranger, Christine, we've been married for nearly thirty years."

"I see your point. Well, if you want to do something which will help you take your mind of things I suppose you could drive me around town and help me look for Clifford."

"Of course I will, Christine." Lydia suddenly forgot about her marital problems and put her closest friend first.

Christine and Lydia set off in search for Clifford. The police had come to the conclusion that Clifford had run away, then they agreed that he had faked his own death or had run off with a mysterious mistress who was seeking a married lover. The only useful thing that the detective inspector did was print Clifford's picture in the local newspaper which was briefly shown on the news.

The afternoon was coming to an end and evening was drawing in. Clifford was still stuck up a tree with the wolves circling. "They're still here," Clifford said bored to death. "I am wasting my life away, plus I am starving. Maybe if I reverse the psychology and chase the wolves." Clifford believed that he had come up with a plan. He jumped down the from tree. "BOO!" he shouted, and the wolves all looked at each other. Clifford ran for his life once more from the bloodthirsty wolves.

As Clifford ran his body finally gave up and he plunged to the ground. The wolves got closer and closer to his weakened body, and Clifford accepted that he had only minutes to live. Then a loud gunshot went off scaring away all the wolves. "Thank you, God!" Clifford muttered, and blacked out.

EIGHT

"Is he dead?" a faint voice said. Clifford felt dazed and lost. He woke seeing people in white coats looking down at him.

"Am I dead and in heaven?" Clifford said, lying lifeless on a bed. Two doctors and an assistant gathered round the bed checking him all over.

"Shhh!" the doctor ordered looking at the assistant. "Melvin, what have I told you about using the word 'dead'?"

Sorry, Doctor Pukka," said Melvin hanging his head like a little child.

"Where am I?" asked Clifford not moving his head and looking at the blurry ceiling.

"It's okay, sir," said the doctor, then he leant towards Clifford.

"You're in a psychiatric hospital."

"But I am not crazy," said Clifford, "I am exhausted from running."

Melvin laughed. "You're not crazy? Why then did a group of fox hunters find you naked in the middle of the forest? You're the meaning of the word crazy."

"Yes, thank you, Melvin," said the doctor, "haven't you got things to be getting on with?"

"Maybe I have and maybe I haven't."

"Just get on with it," said the other doctor.

Doctor Pukka and Doctor Highland discussed Clifford and nurses were called in to deal with his deep wounds. The doctors were unsure if they should class Clifford as insane until one of the nurses recognised him from the news.

"That's the missing man from the town on the other side of the countryside!" she screeched.

"Right," said Doctor Pukka. "Nurse, if you would continue to attend to Clifford I shall ring his home number and inform the person there that Clifford Cockflint is safe and sound and in the care of professionals." With that Doctor Pukka went off to his office leaving a group of nurses to help Clifford recover. They nursed him for an hour and in the meantime Doctor Pukka could not get through to anyone at Clifford's home. Christine was still out looking for him with Lydia. The doctor left a message on the answering machine hoping that Christine would not be much longer. Within a few hours Clifford was sitting upright drinking a cup of tea. Plasters covered his body particularly his feet which had suffered most of the damage. As Clifford sat in bed he noticed that there were a lot of patients wandering the grounds. Some were talking to themselves while others did nothing and just sat there clapping their hands or hiding their faces. Clifford was curious and wanted to explore the hospital so he buzzed to get a nurse's attention.

"Yes, Clifford?" said one of the many nurses in the hospital.

"May I wander the grounds of the hospital in a wheelchair guarded by one of the nurses please?"

"Oh, Clifford, I am not sure about that. Doctors prefer it when the patients stay in their own little corner," said the nurse.

"But I am not a patient," Clifford corrected. "You all thought I was insane when I arrived here."

"Well, I suppose so."

The nurse helped Clifford to a wheelchair. He repeatedly pulled faces showing that he was in pain when he moved. Clifford then went to observe what the patients do while living in a psychiatric ward day in and day out. He noticed that many of them kept themselves to themselves. Clifford was gobsmacked by the amount of adults there ranging from thirty to very elderly. The nurse told him that many were severely depressed and were at risk of committing suicide because a close relative had died, or they felt isolated from the rest of the world as they felt they did not belong. Others were there because life was just too tough for them to handle and had suffered a complete mental breakdown. Clifford came to a ward which distressed him above the rest. It was the number of young people in the ward ranging between fifteen to twenty years old that Clifford found upsetting. They seemed washed out, lost and alone, and it was like an alien had placed some alien children who were not aware of anything logical, or did not understand the meaning of reality. They just sat there in their eerie rooms quietly watching the television but not acknowledging or understanding what was happening in the programme. Some were reading novels. The most important thing for the teenagers to feel was that they were safe in their environment.

"Nurse, they are so young. Why are they here?" asked a shocked Clifford.

"Some came from a poor background that completely messed them up so they could not get on in normal society. The boy in room two had suffered a nervous and mental breakdown over the pressure of his exams."

"Poor lad," said Clifford. "Am I allowed to talk to any of them?"

"Now that, Clifford, I am not sure."

"Look, nurse, I am a teacher, plus the kids may be relieved that they are speaking to an adult who is not a doctor. I promise I will not do anything to upset them."

"Okay, Clifford, you have ten minutes. Why don't you speak to the boy in room two. His name is Chris Frost and all he needs is patience and understanding, so don't upset him."

Clifford wheeled himself into Chris's room. Chris sat there reading a book and his eyes showed that he was absorbed in what he was reading. Clifford took a deep breath and began to talk. "Hi there, what are you reading?" said Clifford kindly. Chris did not reply and carried on reading. "I see you enjoy reading, you seem a keen reader. I love reading too from writers such as Pat Barker, Tom Sharpe or Tolkien, but I do enjoy factual writers like Oliver Sacks or Simon Callow."

Chris stopped reading then moved the book down from his face and closed it. He studied Clifford's face then smiled. "I read a book by Roald Dahl yesterday. I know he is a children's writer but I still enjoy them," said Chris softly. "I am reading about old British steam trains, I love trains, just everything about trains gives me a glorious feeling. Steam train conventions are the best days in the year. I even prefer the conventions to Christmas or my birthday. Well, on my birthday I normally spend my time at the railway conventions. Anyway, do you like trains?"

Clifford was delighted that he had managed to start a conversation with him and answered him with, "Yes, I love trains, particularly the whole nostalgia of the steam era. My wife and I sometimes go on days out on a great steam engine."

"Wow! That's incredible," said Chris.

"I am not a fan of the electric trains," said Clifford.

"Why?" asked Chris.

"Well, a few years ago a stationmaster shouted, 'All aboard, All aboard'. Thousands of hard-working citizens climbed aboard the train during the morning rush hour. I was with my wife Christine and we were on our way back from staying with her mother and we picked the wrong times. The train finally pulled out of the station after being delayed for eighty-five minutes. I sat on an uncomfortable seat next to a noisy lady who was laughing loudly at her book. The rain was thundering against the window but the worst part of the journey was the disgusting coffee. I had bought a cup from the station café and when I sat down and took the lid off the coffee was dirty and there were little bits of something floating on top. I knew it, I absolutely knew when the lady who served me was scratching that greasy hair of hers that dandruff and nits would fall out. Honestly, it seemed that she had washed her hair in a deep fat fryer." Chris was gripped by Clifford's story, and he knew that if he was on that train he would have found the journey distressing. "I started walking around the train looking for some seats for me and Christine to sit. When we moved there was some little pest chucking old sweets and hard bits of chewing gum that he had pulled off from under his seat. There was a lady who looked like a witch because her nose was so long and with the amount of moles and warts that covered her face she was almost hidden… which would have done her a favour. So as you can see, Chris, I am not a fan of modern things including trains. I am more of a steam train man."

"What did your wife think of the journey?" asked Chris.

"She did not enjoy it. She felt unwell after she had bought a cup of tea, and when she got to the bottom of her cup there was someone's fingernail lying there." They both scrunched their faces. "But enough about my experiences, Chris."

"I like hearing about people's stories, even more when it regards trains. I am not a lover of electric trains but from reading history everything based around technology will change."

"Yes indeed, Chris." Clifford took a breather, and he felt guilty that he had always assumed only mentally disturbed people spent their time locked away in psychiatric hospitals. "Have you been on a steam train lately?" asked Clifford.

"I'd love to go on a steam train again, but the doctor said everybody here was too busy to take me. My parents think it is for the best if I stay here for a bit longer."

Clifford felt a surge emotion run through his system. This boy did not seem to have any major troubles. He wanted to free Chris from this cage he was stuck in but knew there must have been more to his problems. Clifford was curious to know if Chris felt under pressure by his presence. He asked Chris if he got on with the other teenagers, but he told him that none of them communicated with each other due to them all having individual problems, so conversations were limited.

"Some young people that are in here have never spoken," said Chris. "Peter, a boy aged fourteen, stays in room three and all the time he has been here I have never heard him speak."

"Why?" asked Clifford curiously.

"Both his parents died in a car crash. One sunny Sunday afternoon his parents went shopping in the high street and said to Peter, 'We will only be about an hour so don't mess up the house too much', and those were their last words. Peter never saw them again."

Clifford felt reduced to tears. This tragedy was almost too much for him but he quickly snapped himself out of it. "Why am I snivelling? Don't be selfish, Clifford," he said to himself.

"Is there anyone you speak to?" asked Clifford.

"Nurse May and you, that's about it," said Chris, who was searching through another pile of books.

"I saw a girl walking along the corridor. Does she live close by?"

"Did she have blonde hair?" asked Chris trying to picture who Clifford was asking after.

Clifford had to think for a moment. "Erm, yes, I think she did," he replied, not entirely confident with his answer.

"Well if it is the girl I am thinking of," said Chris, "her name is Lauren. Now she is a real nutcase," laughed Chris. Clifford popped his head outside the door hoping that Lauren wasn't wandering the corridor and had heard what Chris had said.

"Why is she a nutcase, so to speak?"

"Lauren sniffed too much glue at school. She inhaled too much which inevitably messed with her head leading her to do all kinds of weird things. For example, she entered a building site that was for the construction of a new school. Up the ladder she climbed as she wanted to jump from the highest floor. Of course her aim was not to commit suicide, she just wanted the experience of how it would feel."

Oh crumbs, Clifford thought. Going too high on a trampoline frightened him.

"But her parents visit her regularly," continued Chris.

Clifford wanted to ask Chris about his parents but he refrained from doing so.

The nurse ran towards them to tell Clifford that he would have to leave as the doctor was inspecting the grounds of the children's ward. Clifford told Chris that it was nice meeting him and they exchanged a warm handshake. As the nurse brought Clifford back to his bed Chris poked his head out of the door peering down the hall. He was disappointed that Clifford had to go so soon. After a struggle the nurse managed to get Clifford back into his bed. Doctor Pukka told him that he could not get through to anyone at his house so Clifford knew that Christine would be out looking for him. He asked if he could get a taxi home and just recuperate there. The doctor reluctantly agreed.

After a long day of searching Christine returned home with Lydia. They were both exhausted. "Do you want me to make that tea?" asked Lydia.

"Yes please, you know where all the stuff is don't you?" replied Christine. She walked over to the answering machine and saw that it read one message. She clicked the play button.

It was Doctor Pukka, "Good afternoon, Mrs Cockflint." He was trying not to laugh. "We have your husband here in the psychiatric ward, please feel free to come and see him..." but before the message was finished Christine hung up.

"Quick, Lydia, I need you to drive me to the psychiatric ward, the one beyond the countryside, which is where Clifford has been located. I hope he has not had some kind of mental breakdown."

"He must have bottled up his problems," said Lydia not helping the situation. They dashed to the car and Lydia put her foot down, but just as they drove around the corner a taxi pulled up outside the house.

The taxi driver got out and helped a struggling Clifford to the door. "It's great to be home again. I thought this moment would never happen," said Clifford. He went inside and promised never to take his house for granted again. The hospital had kindly paid for his taxi so the driver left him to get settled in. Clifford sat in his armchair hearing nothing but silence. "Christine," he shouted, "are you upstairs?" There was no reply. He knew she was not there as the house was too quiet. He hoped she would be home soon. Then a car door slammed shut outside. He pulled the net around the window and saw Simon arriving home after his four days away at the Catholic convention. "Blimey, I hope he had a nicer time," laughed Clifford to himself.

Sarah helped Simon with his suitcases. "Oh, Simon, I am so pleased you're home."

"I am glad too, my darling," said Simon. "What have I missed then?"

"You will never believe this, Simon, but Clifford has gone missing."

"Unbelievable," said Simon with a shocked expression on his face. "He was always so careful. May the Lord bless him and keep him safe."

"Christine is so worried."

"I can imagine," said Simon, "I have not visited Christine since she recovered from her illness last year. I will pop in to see her tomorrow."

"That would be nice. Are we going to spend time together?" asked Sarah, desperate for him to say that he'll take her away.

"By the way, Sarah, I am taking a week off work."

"It's a miracle!" said Sarah happily, "Where are we going?"

"No, *we're* not, I am."

"What!" said Sarah in a solemn tone.

"I mean we will of course spend at least one day together, but for the rest of the time I will be away on another religious convention."

"Simon, I am sick of this same conversation being repeated over and over again. This conversation has been repeated more times than *Only Fools and Horses* is on UK Gold."

"Oh, Sarah, don't be like this. We are spending time together now, and then I am off tomorrow."

"But you said you will be visiting Christine tomorrow."

"But I will only be next door."

Sarah knew that she was wasting her breath. "Fine, Simon, fine. I can see that I am not going to win this round." She went upstairs to bed leaving Simon to unpack in his celibate room next door.

Clifford wandered around the house bored out of his brain. He kept thinking about meeting Chris. He wanted to take him on a steam train around Great Britain but he knew that that would never happen, plus he did not think he would see him again.

Meanwhile Christine and Lydia had burst into the psychiatric hospital running as if they were late to a very important meeting with the Queen of England. Christine ran up to the receptionist and banged her hand on the glass of the kiosk. The reception area came to a complete standstill.

"Madam, please be careful, I cleaned the glass an hour ago and your hands are making smudges. I do not want my boss to think that I have been doing nothing all day."

"I am sorry, but I am desperate to be reunited with my husband. It is vital that I speak to Doctor Pukka right this minute!" Suddenly the elevator came crashing down. The cable that made the elevator go up and down had snapped and it landed so hard that smoke appeared when it hit the bottom. The doors slid open and Doctor Pukka rolled out. He staggered across the floor stopping in front of Christine. "He did not have to come that quick," said Christine with a grin.

Doctor Pukka stood up slowly, wobbling from side to side. Two porters brought him a Zimmer frame and Doctor Pukka leaned on it then he walked over to the destroyed elevator shouting up, "Melvin, you have an official warning!"

"Is that officially official by the officials?" answered Melvin.

"I am on the brink of firing you right now," shouted Doctor Pukka.

"How close?" said Melvin cheekily.

"As close as Dick Dastardly and Muttley made it to the finishing line in *Wacky Races*!" roared Doctor Pukka. His face had turned bright red and he looked around him and saw that everybody was staring at him. The smoke had filled the room and people that were sitting waiting patiently began to cough. The nurses went around opening all the windows and kept the main doors opens. Doctor Pukka waved his arms pathetically trying to contribute to clearing the smoke, then he saw a lady standing by reception looking as distressed as a monkey looking for his lost bananas. It clicked that it was Clifford's wife, so he ignored what just happened and went to speak to her. "Are you Mrs Cockflint?" Doctor Pukka said, buttoning up his blazer and pretending to forget that his suit was torn.

"Yes I am," said Christine embarrassed. "Where is my husband?" she said, speaking over the high-pitched laughter because of her surname.

"Your husband," said Doctor Pukka, "left about an hour ago in a taxi. I did ring your home first but Clifford decided to get a taxi."

"Oh what a day," said Christine feeling exhausted, and then her and Lydia left.

Melvin ran down the stairs bumping into Doctor Pukka. They exchanged unpleasant looks. He pointed to the rubble looking at Melvin. "Is this going to clean itself up? I don't think so," said Doctor Pukka sarcastically.

A dull eerie silence filled the house. Once again Clifford began to feel alone, and he contemplated going to see Rufus next door, but he could not risk it in case Christine came home. He rang her mobile phone but she had left it in the bedroom, but he knew Simon would not pop in for a chat and he was not sure whether or not Sarah would be with Christine. Clifford reflected on his past days in the forest. He was unsure of what to do about his car as he was certain that the insurance company would not pay out if he told them what happened. He thought of saying that it had been stolen but then he was worried that the police would be out looking for fictional criminals. He slapped himself and thought that honestly would be the best policy. Then the phone rang and due to the house being eerily silent the volume of the ringtone made a deafening sound. Clifford left it and waited to see if the person would leave a message. It was Rufus who was trying to get through and he left a message. Clifford was not surprised to hear that Lydia had left Rufus a second time in a week. Then he said that he would be staying with his parents, so he cheekily asked Christine if she did not mind watching the house while he was away. Rufus was still unaware of Lydia only being next door as according to him Lydia was at her mother's. Then, to Clifford's amazement, Rufus said, "Hi, Clifford, I know you're home, I saw you getting out of the taxi, answer your bloody phone next time. I'm glad to see you're all right, but don't think I have forgotten that you made me endure the pain of getting a bus. You're a dead man!"

Clifford thought, Ha, typical Jew, misses nothing. As the clock struck eight o'clock he heard the sound of Christine's house key turning in the lock. He turned looking at the front door, then as the door opened Clifford ran and grabbed Christine as she walked in. Then he realised that he had grabbed Lydia because he did not expect her to come through the door. He dropped her on the floor and ran outside as Christine was locking the car door. Christine dropped the keys relieved to see her husband but at the same time shocked to see the state he was in. The reunion had finally come.

"Oh, Clifford, I am sorry for everything."

"Christine, I am sorry for everything too."

"No, no, don't be sorry." They both stared waiting for something to happen.

"Oh, just hug will you for rabbi's sake," interrupted Lydia calling from the front door.

The two embraced each other happily relieved that they were back together. They stood there for a couple of minutes just hugging in their picturesque front garden. They then retreated to the house.

The police called off the search for Clifford as Christine rung them with the good news.

The police and journalists came to interview Clifford, but before that he was in the company of an insurance manager. Even though he said honesty was the best policy he now did not have it in him to say what really happened, plus he did not even tell Christine about the last four days in detail.

"The car was stolen by some thugs, then it was burnt out, destroyed and crushed."

"And where did this happen then, sir?" asked the insurance manager noting what Clifford was staying on his notepad.

"I am not sure," Clifford said, starting to sweat. He did that when he was lying.

"Well then, how did you know what happened to your car after it was stolen?"

"Errr... erm... because they left a random note."

"Can I see it so I can hand it to the police for you?"

"No, no, that won't be possible."

"Why not?" replied the insurance manager curiously.

"The wind blew it out of my hands earlier and it got blown away."

"What wind? There was not a wind four days ago, it was nineteen degrees."

Clifford was running out of ideas, even though nothing he said so far was believable. "Well I am sure the police will find it in a field somewhere."

Just as the insurance manager was about to leave the main office, the person who was in charge of the search came in with some news that did not help Clifford's situation. "Mr Cockflint, your car was found in the river where you crashed it."

"What!" said the insurance manager.

"I'm sorry, I lied because I thought you would not believe me. I did not want you to think that I made the whole thing up as an insurance scam."

"Mr Cockflint, you have completely wasted my time. What really happened?" He was very irritated and Clifford knew it, and his face had changed colour to that of a sunburnt tomato.

Clifford explained the whole story and at the end he had the attention of everyone in the house. The policeman was entranced and the journalist was happy as Clifford's adventures would make a gripping read. Christine carried on with her own things because surreal escapades like this that happened to Clifford did not surprise her one little bit, and realised that this was not going to be the last.

PART TWO

NINE

Clifford and Christine were everlasting lovers. Their affections were as passionate as they had been since they got together. At seventeen they were both intimate for the first time, and many years later their feelings for each other had not changed. Christine always believed that a healthy sex life in a relationship was one of the main reasons that a couple lasted. They never saw intercourse as a chore or as something that a couple had to do because they were married. Sarah and Simon were not lovers at all and Sarah craved Simon's love more than ever, but as Simon was not willing to make love with her she was miserable. Sarah felt unloved and unattractive, she knew that Simon was never going to have sex before marriage but she never thought that she would feel this desperate for him. Christine strongly disliked youngsters sleeping with each other as she only rated sex in proper relationships. Lydia craved intimate love from Rufus but Lydia and even Christine knew the reality of that – it was never going to happen. Rufus was sensitive about his accident and every time he took off his clothes and looked at himself his memories came flooding back. As painful as it is Lydia and Rufus have learnt to accept that sex in their marriage was non-existent.

As a month had passed since Clifford's trauma his wounds were slowly healing. Christine had been absolutely brilliant. She nursed him whenever he needed her, and during that time Christine still carried on with her sessions with Lydia, Sarah and sometimes Rufus, but she was still desperate to speak to Simon. Simon never visited the day after Clifford returned home, his diary was more busier than a politician's diary, but then a bird watcher's diary would be busier than a politician's. Clifford sat in the conservatory with the doors opened outwards onto the garden. All around the conservatory were newspaper articles of his stories stuck on the wall, and there they hung with pride. The public found him fascinating and Clifford never got bored of repeating the same stories over and over again to a new audience.

Clifford had been splashed all over the news, and the reporters and presenters had walked along the field where Clifford's car had left tyre markings. The man that had warned Clifford about the road workings also spoke on the news.

"Oh yes," said one of the men working on the road, "when I spoke to Nicholas I knew that…"

The reporter was waving his arm and whispering quietly to the road builder. "His name is Clifford."

"What?" said the road worker who was now distracted.

"Clifford! Clifford!" said the reporter getting quite distressed.

"You can afford what?" said a puzzled road worker.

"That man's name is Clifford!" shouted the reporter.

"Okay, okay," said the road worker. "Why are you shouting?"

A young tea maker watched this commotion, "Ah, this is professionalism for you," he said quietly to himself.

In other news the BBC spoke endlessly about Clifford. "Hello, my name is Helen Philips. Last night a man who nearly lost his life left a psychiatric ward. It was reported that a group of people had found him naked in the middle of the street. He is lucky to be dead… Oh, sorry, ladies and gentleman, I meant to say alive. Erm, let's go over to our correspondent now and hear from Douglas."

Famous reporter Douglas Chuck was standing in the forest where Clifford had slept. "Thank you and good evening, Helen. Yes, this is one of the many spots where Clifford Cockflint had slept. As you can see it is not fit for human habitation, and how this man survived seems impossible to answer. Also during his few days in the forest he experienced torrential rain. What Clifford experienced really seems so extreme. His wife Christine said during her interview that he has experienced other surreal moments as well. For example…" Douglas opened up a notebook and looked at his notes. "Christine said, 'My husband had been struck by lightning three times while he was walking to Tesco'. Also she said, 'Once he was driving and a man had a heart attack behind the wheel and subsequently died. His vehicle crashed right in front of Clifford's car. Clifford tried to apply his brakes but it did him no favours. Clifford and his car were forced through a massive brick wall, and on the other side was a boat filled with fish, so it was a soft landing. Unfortunately the fishing boat was later hijacked and I didn't see Clifford for two months'." Douglas Chuck looked up into the camera. "I am not making this up. It's totally unbelievable. Christine says, 'When Clifford parked his car one day and then went for a walk, a man put a bomb in the boot of the car. He didn't know who Clifford was, he was just out to cause trouble. As Clifford was heading back to the car a lady's red floppy hat blew off and flew across the car park. Clifford thinking he was being a gentleman gave her his car keys and told her to sit in his car while he went to retrieve the hat. The lady smiled gratefully and off Clifford went. The hat got caught on a tree branch. He grabbed it while the lady was waiting in the front seat. Clifford headed back to the car with the hat held firmly in his hand. BANG! Clifford watched his car blow up in front of him. He was devastated about his car and completely forgot about the lady'." The reporter froze. The cameraman waved his hand to attract Douglas's attention.

"Hello, Douglas, Douglas, please carry on, we are all in suspense of what happens next."

Douglas continued to read his notes. "The police arrested Clifford because from the security footage the police thought the lady's death had been an assassination. Clifford was traumatised for days afterwards, particularly during his murder trial. However, the lady's husband enjoyed the peace and quiet at home so he promised not to press charges." Chuck decided it was time to bring the report to an end. "This is Douglas Chuck, goodnight." He vowed never to meet Clifford just in case things went wrong.

Later that day Clifford had turned off the television. He had heard the news and now he felt tired. He liked to sit in the conservatory which was one of the places where he liked to reflect. The room was cool and Clifford felt at ease. He sat flicking through some articles and laughing to himself. "Well, well," he said, "who would have thought all this attention was coming my way? I certainly did not, especially when I was lost and trapped in that forest out there." On the table there were three big sacks which contained letters from people saying they wanted to meet him. "This is overwhelming," Clifford said to himself.

One of the letters had been written by Rufus. "Why is that man writing to me? He's only next door." Clifford shook his head and put it to one side.

Christine was upstairs listening to Lydia as she once again cried her eyes out about Rufus, their marriage, money and their non-existent loving relationship. Clifford was happy, he had been dealing with people all day and was now thankful for his own space. "Thank the Lord for Lydia's problems, otherwise too many people would be here talking and keeping me and Christine from doing things. The word 'problem' in the dictionary uses Lydia as their example." Suddenly he just stopped talking and stood still, and the only sound that could be heard was the sound of the ticking clock.

Clifford loved life and people, but one of his biggest loves was peace and tranquillity. He lifted the teapot to see if they was any left inside. There was. "Life is all about tea," he laughed to himself. The phone started to ring and Clifford jumped up quickly. "These journalists do not give up." Clifford knew that Christine was working so he answered it. "Hello," he said, excepting it to be another journalist.

"Hello, Clifford, this is the nurse from the psychiatric ward." Clifford was delighted to hear her voice.

"Oh my word, how are you? Clifford could not address her by her name because he could not remember it. How is Chris?"

"Well, that is why I am ringing. It's about Chris, he wants to speak to you."

"Really?" Clifford said happily. He was flabbergasted that Chris took that much of an interest in him.

"He felt comfortable in your company and he has read all of your articles."

"Well... erm... erm..." Clifford could still not remember her name. "Well, my favourite nurse, I'd love to visit Chris. When though?"

"Whenever you're feeling better. I expect it will take some time to fully recover after what you went through."

"I am actually not that bad now, the wounds are healing well."

"Whenever you're ready please could you visit Chris as he has come out of his bubbled world, especially when he talks about the day when he met you." Clifford felt privileged, not only did people respect him for his dangerous four days, but now a young boy with problems attached himself to him. Clifford wanted to visit immediately but he knew that Christine would object, but he was determined.

Sarah's emotions had got the better of her and she was sobbing her heart out in Christine's office. "Oh, Christine, he does not care about me. I can't stand it anymore. I can't marry him. He is so selfish. He lives too much by the book. Suddenly he means nothing to me." Christine was writing down everything that Sarah was saying but she was going too quickly.

"Okay, Sarah, look, just consider this. When you two are married Simon may feel freer to express his love."

"No, I reckon nothing will change. Simon will still work twelve hours then come home and go to his Catholic congregation for two hours every evening."

"Simon is just inexperienced with women, and you are probably his first ever girlfriend…" then Clifford interrupted the discussion.

"Excuse me, sorry about interrupting this gripping conversation but, Christine, I am going out for a few hours." Christine threw her notepad and pencil on the floor.

"No, no, Clifford, I am coming with you."

"No, Christine, I need to go alone."

"Where are you going then?" said Christine running after him and leaving Sarah in the lurch.

"Christine, please, I am going back to the psychiatric ward to see someone that I met."

"Who is that then?"

"He was a young teenager named Chris and he is asking after me, so I want to speak to him and try and get him to open up about himself."

"Okay, I can tell by your face that you are being serious."

"Absolutely serious." Clifford kissed Christine on the lips and then went on his way.

Sarah watched as Christine slowly sunk back into her chair. "He is a good man, Christine, you're very lucky."

"I am a stupid cow."

"Why, because he is visiting a boy in need?"

"No, because I am allowing him to drive our new car." With that the session continued, Sarah talking and Christine distracted by Clifford being out of the house alone.

Clifford drove to the hospital. He had to drive through the countryside as there was not a quicker way. The roadworks had been completed so it was a smooth ride.

Clifford was excited about seeing Chris again. He walked gingerly up to the receptionist who was filing away some important documents. "Excuse me, miss," said Clifford softy tapping his fingers on the glass.

"Don't do that please, sir, everyone seems to like touching the glass and I only cleaned it half an hour ago, so if you wouldn't mind."

"Not at all, miss, I'm sorry, I should have realised."

"That's okay, normally it wouldn't bother me but as the inspector could visit any minute I don't want him thinking I don't do anything all day."

"Yes, yes, I quite understand," Clifford said. "Calm down, love, the inspectors are not going to care about fingerprints on glass." She has an easy life if she is just concerned about dirty windows thought Clifford. He told the receptionist he wanted to see one of the patients. She called one of the nurses and luckily the nurse who spoke to Clifford on the phone came down to meet him.

"Ah, sir, this is Nurse May who will bring you to Chris."

"That was it," said Clifford to himself. "The nurse is called May." He was happy that he could now call her May instead of just plain old nurse.

"How are you feeling. Clifford?" enquired Nurse May "You really did not have to come in today, Chris did not mind waiting a little longer."

"No, no, I am fine thank you," said Clifford. With that Nurse May and Clifford went to see Chris. Chris was in his room going through a load of books that he had read a dozen or so times. Chris liked putting things in piles, he was a person who liked things organised, and if someone messed things up he would not be happy. He felt

62

uncomfortable about the idea of somebody else touching his things without his permission, but people in general knew not to anyway as they knew he would become unhappy. Clifford knocked on his door and said playfully, "Does a Mr Chris live here?"

Chris was delighted to see Clifford.

"Hey, Cliff, you came back." Clifford disliked it when people called him Cliff but it did not bother him seeing that it was Chris. "Hey, Cliff, if I can call you Cliff my name and yours will only have five letters each."

"Oh, you're right, clever thinking, Batman," laughed Clifford.

"What do you mean 'Batman'?" said Chris, who was lost by the remark.

"It's just a phrase which is used by a lot of people."

"I have never heard that phrase before. My parents were not very imaginative." Clifford pondered about the way Chris said things when he was talking. Sometimes he did not look him in the face, other times he went into a daydream or he got up and started putting his books into piles. Chris rearranged some of the books on his desk which included the completed works of William Shakespeare. Clifford asked Chris if he could look inside his copy of his Shakespeare book. Again Chris absolutely hated it when people held his possessions but he allowed Clifford to look at it.

"His completed works, Chris," said Clifford flicking through the pages. "A legendary master of literature. The man was a pure genius."

"*Othello* is his best," said Chris.

"Yes, Chris, I agree with you there. Then it would have to be followed by *Macbeth* or maybe *Romeo and Juliet.*"

"Everybody knows *Romeo and Juliet,*" said Chris. "I suppose it was a compulsory play to read at school."

"I think you're right, Chris."

"*Romeo and Juliet* was the only decent thing I read at school, everything else was rubbish. However, I haven't completed school yet so maybe the class have read some fantastic stuff."

"So, Chris, what have you read lately?"

"Nothing, absolutely nothing, my parents have not brought me anything new to read so I am sitting here wasting my time." The more Chris spoke about his parents the more Clifford wanted to meet them and ask why they had abandoned their son. Clifford observed Chris becoming quite restless. He starting bending his fingers as if he was nervous and his speech went into panic mode until Nurse May went over to him and spoke softly to calm him down.

"Remember, Chris, your parents will see you during the week and bring you many books to read. There will be all kinds of books and you won't be waiting for too much longer." Clifford could see that Chris trusted Nurse May entirely, but he was curious as to why Chris was kept in the psychiatric ward. Nurse May then suggested that a cup of tea would go down a treat, so she left them to go and make it. Clifford told Chris that he would return and that he was going to help Nurse May with the tea. He tapped her on the back.

"Nurse May, why is Chris in here? Please tell me because it seems to me that he should not be. I imagined that all people that live within a psychiatric ward are, I am sorry to be blunt... mentally unstable."

"Everybody thinks that way, Clifford, but I really cannot tell you private information about Chris. This place is all about confidentiality." Clifford looked down at the floor. His eyes appeared to be lost in sadness.

"Look, Clifford, the only person that can tell you anything, anything at all, would be Chris himself."

"Really? Ah, he is a good kid."

"He is," Nurse May agreed. "A really good kid, and his parents are missing out." Nurse may stopped herself from saying anything more just in case she went too far.

The pair of them went back into the room. Chris had started writing in his diary. He kept a lot of diaries as he found that the only person he could share his emotions with was himself by writing down everything in a well-organised, well-kept diary.

"What are you writing there?" asked Clifford with interest.

"It's my diary, I love writing in diaries. It makes me feel intelligent," Chris laughed aloud.

"I agree with you there, Chris, diaries are a good thing, Anne Frank was a lover of diaries."

"Yes, but I don't want mine published. She just wanted to be a future celebrity."

"Is that what you think, Chris?"

"Oh absolutely, there is no doubt about that. I would never want to be a celebrity, I would not be able to handle all the press and people taking pictures all the time. I need my privacy. However, I do like meeting celebrities."

"Oh yes," said Clifford. "And what celebrities have you met?"

"I met J.K. Rowling."

"Really?" shouted Clifford nearly falling from his chair. "That is incredible."

"It wasn't really," said Chris. He was taking about J.K. Rowling as if she was a person working in Sainsbury's. "I told her that she needed to smile more."

"You didn't?" said Clifford.

"I did. Listen, Clifford, she has all the money in the world, she has children, is a worshipped children's novelist and is so miserable looking."

Clifford could not hide the fact that Chris was correct. "Who else have you met?" continued Clifford.

"I met Ringo Starr, and I told him that he should have stayed as the narrator for *Thomas the Tank Engine*. The other narrator was okay but you cannot beat the original." Chris went on guiding Clifford through his adventures with meeting celebrities. "I once told Johnny Depp that he could not act to save his life."

Clifford spat out his tea in shock and it sprayed over the desk. "Wait a minute, wait a minute, Chris. Are you seriously telling me that you told one of America's greatest actors that he should give up the acting business?"

"I absolutely did," said Chris, who was being honest with Clifford.

"And what did Johnny Depp say about that?"

"Funnily enough he agreed," said Chris.

Clifford admired his confidence and his speech. He knew that Chris liked debating his thoughts with other people and was not afraid of defending his opinions.

"What about you, Clifford, have you met any celebrities?"

"Oh crumbs, where do I begin?" said Clifford. "I once met Griff Rhys Jones when he was walking around a car boot sale near to where I live. His voice is something to be desired, it is so unusual. I should have never told him that it sounded worse than a chainsaw."

Chris laughed.

"Griff Rhys Jones then punched me in the face. My wife was horrified but said I deserved it. I fell back onto a table where a woman was selling underwear. She must have thought I was some kind of pervert! Then there was this terrible occasion where I decided to go to a science fiction convention to meet an absolute hero of mine, Mr Chris Barrie. I think he is a legend of his generation. Firstly I dislike science fiction very much, I really do, it is ridiculous, boring and unrealistic, but I do enjoy Chris Barrie in *Red Dwarf*. So anyway, I reluctantly agreed to attend this convention but when I heard who was going I was one hundred per cent chirpy. I could not wait to meet him. However, I was nervous and excited at the same time and I wanted to make a good impression." Chris was engrossed by Clifford's stories and he knew that Clifford had a natural gift for creating an amusing climax.

"Danny John Jules called people in the queue traitors for not queuing for his autograph. Then the person in the front of me was called to meet Chris Barrie and then it was my turn. The moment had come, but, oh dear, I had forgotten all my questions and I spoke like I was having a stroke. My speech was slurred and mumbled. I was completely star-struck. He was in a sitcom called *The Brittas Empire* which was a great comedy and his character in series five got killed from a large, metal, water tank crashing through the ceiling and landing on him, and I stupidly asked him, 'Did you really get crushed by that water tank'?"

"Oh no," laughed Chris. He thought this story was hilarious.

"It gets worse," said Clifford. "After Chris Barrie paused and glared at me as if I was some complete imbecile, he answered my question saying, 'It was done with the aid of special effects'. When I got his autograph, I sat for a while crying like a baby. Then I went back to my car, but as I reversed out of my parking space I knocked my glasses from my face and didn't see a car that was coming out of the space opposite. I crashed into it with such force that the car ended

66

up in a muddy ditch. The person driving turned out to be Mr Chris Barrie himself. He got out of his car but fell down a mud hole and a rescue team had to be called out. However, a railway bridge that went over the ditch suddenly collapsed. It was manic panic for Chris Barrie, then no sooner had he been rescued than an engine veered off the track and came crashing down on top of Chris Barrie's car. I can safely say, Chris, that Chris Barrie did not, and has not, forgotten who I am. I now have a police restriction saying that I am not allowed to be within ten miles of him." Both Clifford and Chris felt exhausted after that story and had a cup of tea.

The rest of that day Clifford and Chris spoke in detail about celebrities, politics and education. They both learnt a lot from each other but as time was getting late Clifford knew that Christine would be worried, especially now that her day of work was over and Lydia would probably be in the bath leaving Christine alone with her thoughts. So Clifford called it a day.

TEN

Christine had prepared dinner. She sat on the sofa eating her favourite dish, chicken curry. Lydia had gone to see her mother for the evening as she always made time for her during the week. Christine loved having the house to herself for a little while as it was the only chance she had to catch up on her programmes. She enjoyed the soaps and reality shows. Clifford disliked her programmes therefore he would go upstairs and read the latest novel that he had bought. Sometimes he would go into the attic and organise all his jumble. His attic was a storage holder, but Clifford refused to sell any of his things as could not bear to be parted from anything. His books were all around the room on the floor. Clifford had put up shelves around the room, but there was still not enough space for all his 'gorgeous books' as he would say. In the centre of the room were three enormous tables that had been pushed together so Clifford could create his dream railway. He had built model houses, a church and a library that looked like the White House. He had built a hill in the centre of his train set and on the top of that hill was his house and his neighbours' houses. Everything was perfect, there was not one thing out of place, and even the grass was level. His mother in law had said that if he had to sacrifice his hobbies room or Christine she was positive that Christine would be shown the door. At this precise moment, however, Clifford was not concentrating on his trains as he was looking for books that he thought Chris would enjoy.

Christine had made Clifford a plate of chicken curry and she had kept it warm for him in the oven. Clifford went into the living room.

Clifford and Christine are very house proud and they had renovated the living room, indeed the whole house, when they moved in. The living room was like a cess pool as a group of drug dealers lived their previously. Clifford and Christine loved the house so much that they were not going to allow the state of the living room to stop them buying their dream home. After they had spent thousands renovating the living room it was unrecognisable. A room that had looked worse than the trenches had been completely transformed. It was now in pristine condition and they kept it that way.

"Something smells gorgeous. Lydia must be out of the house."

"Oh, Clifford, don't be wicked, your dinner is in the oven."

"I'm only joking, love." Clifford went into the kitchen and pulled out his dinner. "Blimey, your curry smells nicer and nicer every time."

"Thank you, dear, I'm just watching *Coronation Street*."

"Has it been on long?" Clifford was hoping that she would answer 'nearly finished'.

"Part two has just started."

"Oh brilliant," Clifford answered sarcastically.

As he started eating he thought about Chris in the hospital waiting for his parents to bring him some books and never turning up. With that Clifford stopped eating his dinner went into the attic to sort out all his books. He filled two bags full of books that he thought Chris might like then put them next to the front door for the following day.

When *Coronation Street* was over, Clifford spoke to Christine about Chris. Christine had always been aware that Clifford was a massive talker but she had never heard him burble on in this manner. He did not acknowledge Lydia tripping over the books when she came in. Clifford went on and on until he had finished.

"You find this boy interesting then, Clifford?" said Lydia with a hint of sarcasm.

"Where is Rufus? I am beginning to miss that man."

"He is probably next door. Only the rabbi knows what he is doing."

"Maybe he has a secret woman with him."

Lydia laughed while looking at Clifford and thinking that even the stupidest person in the world would not have said something that stupid.

"What? Are you actually referring to my husband, my husband Rufus Feldman? The man who can't even tell the difference between a man and a woman?" Lydia laughed again hysterically.

"So what did Rufus think you were then, Lydia? Maybe he bats for the other side, and when he found out you were a woman that's the reason your sex life is crap."

Christine put her hand over her mouth in horror. She had never heard Clifford answer someone like that before.

"You're really annoying me tonight, Clifford!" said Lydia. "If I find out that Rufus really does have a woman with him I will go mental."

"Oh, Lydia, think nothing of it, I wasn't being serious."

"No, but I am," said Lydia. She shot up quicker than someone being shot out of a cannon and ran home to her husband.

"You surprise me sometimes, Clifford," said Christine.

"I surprise myself," agreed Clifford. The room went silent for a bit, then Clifford looked at Christine.

"Do you fancy sex?" he said bluntly.

"What type of sex?" Christine replied.

"A 90s film theme. I'll wear my Fred Flintstone costume because it's easy to take off…"

"I'll wear my Mrs Doubtfire suit," said Christine.

"This dressing up thing gets weirder and weirder every time," said Clifford.

The next morning the Cockfields woke feeling refreshed and revitalised. Christine made breakfast and Clifford opened the post. Clifford ate slightly quicker than usual as he was looking forward to going to see Chris and give him his books.

"Clifford, I'm thinking about doing a dinner party for our neighbours. It'll be a nice get-together."

"That is a good idea. Let's just hope we get them all here together, you know what Simon is like."

"If I ring Sarah personally she could ask him tonight."

Christine loved cooking meals for her neighbours. She enjoyed cooking in general but making a meal and dessert for good friends was the highlight of her week. Although it was not easy she had to make a separate meal for Lydia and Rufus, Sarah was allergic to a lot of ingredients Christine used and Simon was a vegetarian. Despite this Christine still aimed to please her guests, and after twenty years of cooking not a single complaint was said to the chef… just behind her back.

No sooner had Clifford left for the hospital, Sarah popped in from over the fence to see Christine. "Morning, Christine!" she shouted. Christine unlocked the back door.

"Morning, Sarah, come in, I was just making some coffee. Would you like a cup?"

"I could never turn down one of your coffees," said Sarah. "So have you planned any more for Lydia and Rufus's thirtieth anniversary for next week?"

"Absolutely, Sarah. I have nearly done everything. I am planning an evening meal for us all. It's about time we all had a get-together."

"Brilliant idea, Christine."

"Lydia and Rufus may not appear to be the happiest couple in the world, but they should be happy next week."

"Their thirtieth. I can't believe it."

"Make sure Simon comes to this dinner please."

"I'll do my best," said Sarah, already predicting the answer.

Lydia popped her head through the back door. "Can I come in?" she said having already walked into the kitchen and helping herself to some coffee. "I needed to come over. Rufus did not go into work today because of some stupid cold. It's not even that serious, but I won't be spending time with him as I don't want to get it."

"You just said it was nothing serious," said Sarah.

"Yes, but whenever I catch something off Rufus I always seem to get it a hundred percent worse." Lydia was of course exaggerating. She did this frequently even though she was kind to her friends and craved love from Rufus, but she had no sympathy for him when he was unwell. Back in 1983 Rufus was rushed into hospital with appendicitis and it was vital he had an emergency operation otherwise it could have been fatal. Once again Lydia refused to visit him because she was worried her appendix would need removing. The doctor explained to her on the phone that you cannot catch appendicitis like you can a cold, but she refused to be told and left him in the hospital alone for three days.

"Simon never takes a day off sick. I cheekily asked him to pull a false sickie and he then picked up a glass of holy water and threw it over me saying the Lord's Prayer. I was furious, he is such a drama queen. Then we both realised that it was a Sunday and he didn't even work on a Sunday."

"Lydia, I am planning a dinner party which will happen sometime this week, probably Friday, so please keep it free."

"I can't wait but please remember to cook kosher food."

"Lydia, for the past twenty years you have said that to me and I haven't once cooked anything for you non-kosher, have I?"

"No, sorry, I'll leave you to it," said Lydia.

Lydia and Sarah left. Neither of them had a session today therefore Christine had a free day.

Meanwhile Chris went through Clifford's books. "I have not read any of these books."

"Neither have I, Chris," said Clifford.

"Why did you buy them? Isn't it a waste of money?" said Chris who was confused.

"No, not at all. A book lover will buy a book sometimes simply because of the appearance of it."

Chris found Clifford a very interesting person and they spoke more personally about their lives. Clifford told Chris that his wife Christine had been very ill and that was the reason he had time to see him was because the school agreed for him to take a year off. Chris finally came clean about the reason he was living at the psychiatric ward. Chris explained that when he was younger his mother had told him that a doctor had diagnosed him with Asperger's syndrome. It had hit him hard even though his mum had told him that the diagnosis was very mild. The point was he still had the condition. He was upset by this and felt very insecure. He thought people would notice if he did something strange, but people thought him a normal person. For years no one ever suspected anything, he had got on with everybody, he excelled with his social skills and was a diligent student. However, the only time Chris seemed to have problems was when he struggled to understand the simplest instructions or if anything had to be done precisely or immediately. If something got messed up or he made a mistake which disrupted his schedule, Chris would have a breakdown over it and could not cope with the aftermath. Then one day, six years after finding out about his

Asperger's, someone found out about it and then everyone in his year knew. When Chris knew he had been found out he was horrified by the thought of everyone knowing and ran out of school. Chris's biggest fear was being treated differently by other children because of the way he was, and now they knew his secret. He could not handle it. Furthermore which didn't help was his parents never fully understood the diagnosis and chose to ignore Chris's needs. Finally, after two difficult days, Chris collapsed after a mental breakdown and his parents were told it was best if he was placed in a psychiatric ward until they felt he was okay to be released. Chris's parents thought it would be better for him to remain at the hospital, but this was the worst thing they could have done.

Clifford felt deeply emotional about Chris's predicament and he decided that he would stand in as his substitute parent. Nurse May brought in some tea and Clifford whispered to her that Chris had told him everything. She was amazed by this. Even though she knew that Chris and Clifford had bonded, she never thought he would have told him this soon. Clifford left Chris with his books and told him that he could take his time with them.

"You are a walking miracle, Clifford," said Nurse May astonished.

"Why?" questioned Clifford.

"Chris has never told a living soul that story of his past."

"He is a good child, Nurse May, and he needs to be acknowledged by people from the outside world. He has been cooped up in here for a year. By the way, how often do his parents visit him?"

Nurse May thought about that and the duration of time told Clifford that they did not visit enough.

"That's disgusting, Nurse May, if you cannot even remember the last time his parents visited. Nurse May, I want to take Chris out and about to see places and to have a bit of a life."

"Look, Clifford, if I have to be honest I don't think the doctors will allow you to take one of our patients…"

"He is not a patient, he is a student," Clifford snapped.

"Sorry, Clifford, but whatever you say it's down to the doctor's consent before you do anything."

"Right then, I want an emergency appointment with Doctor Pukka please."

"Wait here, I'll see if Doctor Pukka is free." Nurse May was slightly taken aback by Clifford's tone. She tapped on the glass to get the receptionist's attention.

"PLEASE, PLEASE, PLEASE, don't touch my windows. I only cleaned them half an hour ago. What do you think the inspector would say if he came in? He might think I do nothing all day."

Just then the highest inspector of hospitals in Great Britain and Northern Ireland walked into the hospital and straight up to the receptionist. "I have never seen such dirty windows in all my years of being an inspector." The receptionist crumbled. "What the hell do you do all day, doss?" The receptionist saw bright red, unlocked herself from the ball that she crawled into and standing to be seen by everyone she picked up her computer chair and threw it through the glass window. The glass shattered into tiny pieces which covered the floor.

"You hate dirty windows," she said sharply as she tossed the cloth into the inspector's left hand. "You bloody clean the windows, you prick." She stormed out of the hospital then walked back in because she had forgotten her handbag.

Clifford marched into Doctor Pukka's office demanding that Chris has more freedom from the hospital. The doctor was aware that Chris was cooped up far too much in his room. Doctor Pukka explained to Clifford that Chris had been offered to be taken for a walk in the past, but had refused. Nurse May offered to go with him but Chris still did not feel he could trust her. Doctor Pukka told Clifford the only way he would be able to take Chris out of the hospital for a while would be if he was a psychiatric volunteer. The doctor told Clifford that he did not need to become a full-time volunteer, but could do the hours that suited him. Clifford had taken a year off to spend time with Christine so he knew that when he was choosing his hours he needed to put her first.

It was finally agreed that Clifford would work for two hours on a Monday afternoon, Thursday Morning and then on a Sunday if Chris wanted to go out. Sunday was not compulsory. Nurse May took Clifford into the staffroom to get him a white coat. It was essential that Clifford had his picture taken, so he could get in using a swipe card. Afterwards she gave him an orientation of the hospital Clifford did not get shown, not just around the children's ward but also adults with more than just depressive problems.

At the end of the day Clifford signed out, and as he walked over to his car he heard a knocking sound. He turned to see who was trying to get his attention. Chris was standing at his window waving goodbye to Clifford, and he held up one of the books to establish that he was enjoying the read.

On the way home Clifford was contemplating on how to build up Chris's confidence with people. He knew that Chris felt comfortable in his company, and he also knew that was due to the bonding time they had together. Once again Clifford took another route home and he watched other people walking. Some were walking with friends, others were walking with their parents and some couples were just strolling around. Sadness started to get hold of Clifford as he thought Chris would never experience these types of things with people if he was too afraid to step out of the ward. Then as he drove further through the town it suddenly occurred to him that he knew a perfect place to take Chris. It was not too far from the hospital and it would be a place Chris would feel secure and confident. Clifford pulled up by the side of the road.

"Why did I not think of this place earlier?" he said slapping his head.

ELEVEN

Lydia and Rufus were sitting back to back in Christine's kitchen refusing to talk to each other. Lydia held her nose in the air and Rufus did not give a crap on how his wife was feeling. "Now come on, you two, just talk to one another," said Christine. "You're acting like children."

"You must be joking," said Rufus. "Jewish children don't act like this. Lydia is really bringing my status down."

"Shut up, Rufus! You cannot take it that Topshop clothes suit my figure."

Rufus laughed and said, "Ha, what figure? Saggy and lanky."

"In all the years we have been married you have never behaved this appallingly."

"Is there a point in this marriage?" asked Sarah, who was sitting at the breakfast table observing the scenario.

"Of course. Well we are not getting a divorce," said Rufus. "Divorce is not very Jewish, and not to mention the cost."

"Oh, forget our Jewishness, Rufus. I think we should separate."

"No, Lydia, things are not that bad."

"Not that bad? Rufus, are you stupid? I dread to think what our relationship would be like if it was bad," said Lydia.

"Listen," interrupted Christine, "I've planned to do our dinner evening tomorrow. We can all have an adult conversation and see how things go."

"The good news is my devilishly handsome fiancé Simon will be able to come tomorrow," Sarah said happily.

Rufus and Lydia reluctantly nodded and Lydia said they would be there at eight o'clock.

That night Rufus did something that surprised Lydia. He went over to the cabinet and took out three photo albums dated from when they first met till now. Lydia didn't even realise that Rufus knew the photo albums existed. They both laid in bed rekindling memories. "Look, Lydia, this was the time when you met the American actor Michael Keaton at the West End production of *Hamlet*."

"Oh yes, he was a decent bloke," said Lydia holding the picture away from her face because she was finding it difficult to see. "Even my eyesight is failing me now. This picture of me with Michael Keaton makes me realise that I am getting old."

"Lydia, you're as young as you feel," said Rufus reassuringly.

"You've changed your tune," said Lydia finding Rufus's sudden change of heart a little strange.

"Look, let's go to the dinner party tomorrow and enjoy the company."

"Your right," said Lydia, and kissed Rufus on the cheek.

"I hope Simon doesn't start talking his Catholic crap."

"Rufus, please don't ruin a good moment," said Lydia, and she kissed him again. The lights went out and they went to bed.

Clifford and Christine were lying in bed. Christine was watching the late movie on the upstairs television which hung on the wall, while Clifford was reading a book on Asperger's syndrome. During the evening Clifford told Christine that he had volunteered at a psychiatric ward. She thought that what he was doing was out of kindness. Then the film finished and Christine wanted to go to sleep.

"Can I turn the light off please, Clifford?" asked Christine who was going to turn off the light anyway.

"Wait a minute, Christine, I have nearly finished this chapter."

"Clifford, get a kindle, that would make things so much easier."

"No way, I absolutely despise kindles. What is the point of reading a book if you cannot hold the book itself?"

Clifford finished reading the current chapter and Christine then turned the light off. She climbed into bed and cuddled up to Clifford. "I have made up a menu for tomorrow night."

"Lovely, what is for pudding?"

"Trifle of course."

"Yes, I love trifle."

"I know, that's why I made it. When are you next seeing Chris?"

"On Sunday, it will be the first time Chris will leave the hospital."

"You're a really kind man," said Christine as they both drifted off to sleep.

Sarah went to bed alone. Simon was in the next room saying his night prayers which usually took about forty-five minutes. He did this every single day without failure. Never in a month of Sundays would Simon ever forget. Then to Sarah's annoyance he would sing a hymn. When he was finished he would shout, "Goodnight, Sarah, God bless," but Sarah would have fallen asleep the minute Simon had finished singing.

Friday afternoon and the Cockflint's kitchen is manic with Christine cooking all sorts of meals. Her group of friends were fussy eaters but Christine was determined to get it right. For herself and Clifford she cooked a shepherd's pie, for Sarah fish and chips, just chips for Simon, and for Lydia and Rufus roasted chicken with potatoes. It had proven to be an extremely challenging day for Christine. Clifford was looking through the wine cupboard. He did not enjoy being in the company of people who drank but it never bothered his friends who were drinking around him. Christine had not cooked a candlelight supper for a few years, so the wine bottles in the cupboard had increased from two to seven bottles. There was a mixture of red and white wines and Clifford called them the ladies' drink.

Since Lydia had hit the menopause she could not handle her drink as well as she used too. Sarah was young and still enjoyed socialising with her friends in the local clubs. However, since Christine's illness last year she had stopped drinking completely. She had never been a heavy drinker in the first place but she did enjoy a get-together with her friends along with a few glasses of wine. Simon drank red wine but he always said a quick prayer before each gulp. Rufus did not drink as he found wine too expensive, and he even refused to buy the cheap wines from Lidl. Every now and then Lydia would purchase the odd bottle when Rufus irritated her, or when she looked in the mirror and reminded herself that she was old.

Christine was cooking the food and everything was going to plan. Everything was on schedule which gave Christine plenty of time to start making her famous trifle. After she made it she put it in the fridge to set then sat down to take a break.

"Clifford have you chosen the wines yet, you've been looking in that cupboard for ages? Thank the Lord you are not cooking these meals otherwise we would not be eating till tomorrow night."

"Ah, Christine, should I bring all the bottles out and let the guests choose what they want?"

"Yes, that sounds like a good idea," said Christine as she took a mouthful of tea.

"Is there any tea left in the teapot?" asked Clifford. "How are you feeling, my love, you're not stressed are you?"

"No, no, not in the slightest, but I just want to make sure everything goes according to plan."

"Of course it will, my love, I'll be with you. Just make sure Rufus and Simon don't sit next to each other."

"Yes, good point," agreed Christine.

They both got caught up in conversation and Christine did not realise that steam was seeping out through the oven door. She then saw through the reflection of Clifford's spectacles the steam that was filling the kitchen. "ARGH! My Jewish dish!" Christine ran to the oven, put her oven gloves on, and pulled out the food. The gloves were not protective enough and she burnt her hand. "Ouch! My hand," she squealed. She dropped the roasted chicken on the floor and it hit the ground with a splat.

"Oh no, now what?" Christine said in distress, rubbing sweat from her head. Her face had gone bright red. "I have not got time to cook another one."

"Don't cook another one," said Clifford.

"You're not helping, Clifford," said Christine, trying to think of an alternative.

"No, my point is what the eaters don't know won't hurt them."

"What do you mean?" said Christine curiously.

"Well, instead of cooking another roasted chicken which will probably cause you to have a nervous breakdown, why don't you scoop up all the chicken pieces, wash off all the excess bits of dirt, then attempt to mix it up in the potatoes and say it's your own dish?"

"Clifford, are you crazy? My friendship with our neighbours is built on a foundation of trust, and I cannot in any way go behind their…" Silence. "You're a genius, Clifford, help me pick up all the chickens pieces, and make sure there is not a speck of chicken left on the floor."

"I'll get the bucket and mop to wash the floor," said Clifford. "Blimey, it feels like we have committed a murder and we're trying to hide the evidence," he laughed.

"If Rufus and Lydia find out about this they will be committing the murder," said Christine, feeling nervous. After picking up all the chicken they analysed it carefully.

"I don't see anything on it," said Clifford. "Actually, is that dust?"

"Excuse me," said Christine, not impressed by Clifford's remark, "I vacuum every day."

Christine got the dish which had the potatoes in, added the roasted chicken and mixed up everything within the dish. Christine then added more olive oil to wash away any other bits that might have been on the floor. Lastly she put tin foil over the dish and left the chicken till it was ready to dish up. The other food was fine but Christine felt guilty about feeding Rufus and Lydia food that had been on the floor.

"I feel so guilty," said Christine, with an expression on her face that made her look like she should be on *Crimewatch*.

"You shouldn't feel guilty because I don't," said Clifford.

"But you're not the chef!" shouted Christine, annoyed at his insensitive remarks.

"Okay, Christine, I can see you're feeling uncomfortable, I won't say another thing. Discretion is my middle name," laughed Clifford.

"You're acting like Rufus tonight. It must be something to do with age," said Christine.

"I hope not. That means in three years' time you'll be like Lydia."

"My word, it's scary thinking how people can change within a few years," said Christine, contemplating what the future would be like.

"Listen, Christine, Rufus and Lydia must have always been in their mid-fifties with the way they carry on from when we first met them."

"I suppose your right, we'll just have to wait and see," said Christine as she kissed Clifford on the cheek.

The clock struck six o'clock, so the two of them went upstairs to get changed into their evening wear. Clifford loved wearing his tuxedo and the reason he liked it when people came round for dinner was for an excuse to wear it. Clifford would stare at himself in the mirror and say that he was better looking than any James Bond there had been. Christine wore her long, black silk dress and they both looked fantastic. The house was immaculate and there was not a speck of dust in sight.

Before the guests arrived Clifford took it upon himself to ring Chris to see how he got on with his books. Chris said that he enjoyed them all and this made Clifford happy. Although he was disheartened at the fact that Chris's parents had still not spent time with Chris in the hospital, he was beginning to think that they did not care about him, therefore Clifford was beginning to doubt their existence or even if they cared for Chris. Questions were flying around his head as to why the parents were constantly absent at one of the most unhappy times of his life, the time when he needed them the most.

The conservatory was the place where Clifford did all this thinking. He went there when he needed to get his head around things. Sometimes he sat there just thinking how lucky he was to have Christine, but since he had met Chris he had spent more hours in his armchair which was placed in the corner of the conservatory just contemplating Chris's life. He pondered all the advantages and disadvantages of seeing Chris more regularly, and the questions he would ask his parents as to why they don't see him every day.

The sound of the doorbell echoed through the house grabbing the attention of the Cockflints. Christine approached the door adjusting her earrings. "Coming, coming," she said, striding to the door.

"Good evening," said Sarah, "Simon is bringing the drinks in."

"Oh, Simon, you shouldn't have," said Christine.

Simon stood in the doorway, he was tall with blonde hair and gleaming white teeth, and was a very handsome sight indeed. "This lovely drink is for me only, the priest gave it to me, he brought it back from holy grounds."

"Lovely," said Christine. Then she grabbed him by his collar and pulled him down to face level. "Now, Simon, two things. One, I do not want any mention of religion this evening, and if you even mention a word from the bible you'll be eating your dinner in the garden. Two, I want to see you here bright and early in the morning for a session. It'll only be for an hour so I want you to show up, and by God, if you do not turn up you'll be meeting God personally."

"Christine, I have never seen this side to you."

"Well, I have been planning this meal for days and if it is messed up because of you, trust me, you'll know what pain means. Do not think I am being unfair towards you because I will be having the same discussion with Rufus when he arrives. Have a nice evening," said Christine, gently smacking Simon's cheek.

Simon felt nervous. Christine's split personality had not shown before, so Simon knew she was not joking. He quickly ran home and popped the bottle of holy water through the gap from where he had left the downstairs window open.

As Simon and Sarah were settling in the living room, Sarah with a glass of red wine and Simon with a glass of water, Rufus and Lydia arrived.

"Now Christine are you sure the food tonight is Jewish friendly?" asked Rufus.

"Yes, Rufus, of course it is," replied Christine.

Lydia took off her coat and went into the living room. Christine quickly grabbed Rufus by the collar. "Two things," said Christine, staring into the eyes of Rufus. "One, don't you dare upset Lydia tonight, don't belittle her, don't show her up in company and certainly stay off all jokes about age. That's one. Now, number two, if you dare mention any religious details about the Jewish faith tonight over dinner and start an argument with Simon, you'll be back in your house quicker than you can stay rabbi. Do I make myself clear? Have a nice evening."

Rufus never thought he would have felt threatened by Christine, and he did not want to see more of her threatening side, therefore he ran back home and dumped copies of *The Jewish Chronicle* on his sofa.

It was an hour into the night and the six of them mingled comfortably in each other's company. Lydia was helping herself to her fourth glass of wine. "Don't fill up with wine, Lydia," said Christine, "dinner will be ready to dish up soon."

Lydia giggled quietly while Clifford, Rufus and Simon were in the kitchen debating whether or not violence should be shown on television.

"Violence makes good television," said Rufus.

"No, no, no, violence should not be shown or read by anyone anywhere," said Simon.

"Of course you would say that," said Rufus.

"Why?" said Simon.

"Well, you know why, church boy."

Simon was about to let rip into Rufus, but Christine popped her head into the kitchen looking as annoyed as an old person who had their bus pass stolen from them. Rufus and Simon went ghostly pale and not a sound escaped from their mouths.

"Are you both all right?" asked Clifford, who was confused as to why Rufus and Simon went quiet all of a sudden.

"You've got a tough woman, Clifford," said Simon, who was frightened to say anything aloud.

"Who, Christine?" said Clifford, who laughed at Christine being labelled tough, a side to which had been absent in their marriage. "Christine is as soft as a pillow."

Rufus and Simon looked at each other each knowing Christine's hidden personality.

"Okay, everybody, dinner is served!" said Christine.

All the guests claimed their seats choosing to sit with their loved ones. Rufus was about to sit with Clifford but then Christine sneakily pushed him down to the next chair so he would be sitting with Lydia. Everybody started to eat and the meals were going down a treat. Simon was very satisfied with his plate of fish and chips; eating no meat made him happy. Rufus noticed that it was only his fourth mouthful when he picked out the second strand of hair. He held it up next to Lydia to see if her hair was falling into his dinner but it was not one of hers. However, he noticed that Lydia pulled a strand of hair out of her mouth. Once again he saw another hair hidden within the roasted chicken. Quietly Rufus nudged Lydia to get her attention, and as she looked at him she saw him point at his plate where the hair was. Rufus casually moved his eyes to the plates of his friends, and their plates appeared to be free from hairs. Rufus and Lydia stopped eating and it became obvious that there was a problem.

"Are you all right?" asked Clifford.

"Is the food okay for you both?" said Christine.

"It's lovely," said Lydia. "Isn't it, Rufus?" tapping his arm.

"Ye..." said Rufus who did not even finish his word.

Lydia picked up her fork and started to eat miniature pieces of food while holding a fixed smile.

"My word, that is good food," said Lydia who couldn't be more false.

Rufus put a big piece of food in his mouth then pretended that he needed to blow his nose so he could spit it out. Bit by bit Rufus spat his food into a napkin, and after a while it was full of it. Slowly he unbuttoned his shirt from the bottom of his waist and popped the napkin into the inside of his shirt and buttoned it back up.

"Will you all excuse my rudeness but I'm afraid I need to use the lavatory." Lydia could tell by the use of Rufus's vocabulary that he was up to something. Rufus went to the toilet upstairs and ran over to the tap to rinse his mouth with cold water. Rufus opened the toilet seat and poured the napkins – which now numbered thirteen – down the toilet. Rufus flushed the toilet. It appeared that all the napkins were being flushed away and sent down the sewer, however, the water in the toilet started to overflow pouring out onto Rufus's feet... including the napkins.

"Oh crap!" said Rufus panicking, knowing that the water could ruin the floor, but if in time the water did not stop it could ruin the whole house. Rufus, in panic, saw a bag of toilet rolls by the door and threw five rolls down hoping that they would block the water off, but it only made it much worse. As time went on the water started to seep out from out the door of the bathroom and ran down into the hallway. Rufus caught his shirt on the window handle and as he pulled it off it ripped. Then he dropped it in the puddle of water.

Christine had noticed that Rufus was taking his time. "Is Rufus all right, Lydia?" asked Christine.

"I'm not sure. If you'll excuse me I'll go upstairs and see if he is okay." Lydia excused herself from the table. She had an inkling that Rufus would be in the toilet. Lydia then felt the damp on the carpet outside the bathroom. Her feet squelched in the water and now Lydia was panicking knowing that Rufus had done something.

"Rufus, what are you doing in there?" she said, hammering on the door.

"Just having a wash," replied Rufus, saying the first stupid thing that came into his head.

"Don't be silly, Rufus, what are you doing in there!" said Lydia, wanting to shout, but she did not want to draw attention from the people downstairs.

Meanwhile, at the dinner table, Clifford felt a slight twinge. "Excuse me, everyone, a call of nature," said Clifford dying to use the toilet. He saw Lydia standing outside. "Oh dear, is there a queue for the loo?"

"Oh, Clifford!" shouted Lydia.

"What is going on?" asked Clifford curiously.

"Nothing, nothing," said Lydia, faltering.

"Lydia, I can tell by your actions that something is..." Clifford looked down at the carpet. He could see water swimming around his toes.

"Why is there water all over my lovely carpet?" Clifford said waving his hands around.

"Rufus has had an accident with your toilet. It's being an awkward and difficult toilet."

"Oh, don't patronise me with your rubbish, Lydia," said Clifford, and opened the door of the bathroom. Water burst through the open door and plunged down the stairs like a waterfall.

Clifford grabbed Rufus by the scruff of the neck. "Rufus, what the hell have you done to my house?"

Rufus started wailing like a child who had lost his favourite toy. "But, Clifford, the water... I didn't know... everything happened to quickly... no one helped..."

"Oh stop snivelling, you little man. You are going to pay for this damage. Jew or non-Jew you will write a cheque out for me when we somehow stop this water from running all over the house." At that moment the door closed behind Rufus, Lydia and Clifford. Lydia made a grab for the doorknob but it fell off and the three of them were trapped inside the bathroom with the water running.

"What are we going to do?" said Clifford in a frenzy, frantically trying to think of a solution, but the sense of panic was distracting him.

"Calm down, Clifford, everything will be okay," said Lydia, who knew very well that everything was not okay. The water was pouring out of the toilet so fiercely that it was beginning to ruin the bathroom floor.

Christine went into the kitchen to make coffee for everyone, but as she started drops of water started to drip onto her shoulder. At first she did not notice the water dripping through the gap in the floorboards, but eventually she felt the dampness on her.

"What in the world?" Christine said to herself, then she looked up at the ceiling, realising that the ceiling was about to cave. Christine screamed and threw herself out of the kitchen landing on her front. Simon and Sarah jumped up to help her when suddenly the bathroom floor ended up in the kitchen including all the water, Rufus, Lydia, Clifford and the wrapped up bits of food in the napkins. Christine's dream kitchen had been destroyed. She walked into the kitchen ankle high in water ignoring Rufus, Lydia and Clifford who were flapping about on the floor like fish out of water. She took the trifle out of the fridge then walked back into the dining room and placed it on the table. Christine sat down and froze.

Clifford desperately tried to make himself look presentable, unfortunately his spectacles fell off in the crash and were lost under all the rubble. Bits of the ceiling had lodged deep in Lydia's hair including a couple of napkin balls. Rufus had landed in the corner with the toilet sitting on his lap.

"Christine, I can explain!" said Clifford raising himself and trying to get to Christine's level. Christine appeared to be dazed, lost in a parallel universe. Simon and Sarah were speechless, they were unaware of what was going on upstairs.

"Christine, this is all Ruf..."

Rufus jumped to his feet. He was worried about Christine's reaction. "Oh, Christine, I feel that I must apologise for my wife's clumsiness," Rufus lied, happy for Lydia to take his blame.

"You what!" said Lydia, picking out some of the ceiling from her hair.

"Yes, yes, I'm afraid Lydia is not... is not... well, in a sense not very good with technical machinery."

"A toilet is not technical machinery," snapped Lydia.

"Words of an amateur. Of course lavatory flushing systems are technical machinery," Rufus rumbled on.

"Don't worry, Clifford and Christine, I'll pay for this mess, I don't mind paying for my old bird's catastrophic clumsiness." Lydia opened her right hand, stretched her finger out wide placing her hand around the crown of Rufus's head and pushed with all her might until his face plunged into the bowl of trifle. Lydia then took an unopened bottle of wine and went upstairs. After laying there for a few seconds Rufus picked his head up out of the trifle. Clifford got up from the floor and Christine could not even look at him because she was so disgusted with his lies. Christine knew that Lydia had not caused the mess.

"You know," said Rufus, spitting some of the trifle out of his mouth, "I think I have managed to upset some people tonight."

TWELVE

That night Christine was ordered to go to bed due to her shock at what had happened. Clifford had called a doctor who said she was to stay in bed and rest. The kitchen, the toilet and the upstairs hallway were completely destroyed.

Rufus went home and thought he would hide away until the dust had settled. Lydia was nowhere to be seen and Simon ordered Sarah to go home because he felt that the house was too dangerous to be in. For hours during the night Clifford and Simon were clearing away the mess. The workmen were due for arrival in the morning, however, they both thought that it would be better if they made a quick start. Time was ticking and Clifford was thinking about Christine, so he told Simon that he was calling it a night. Simon told Clifford that he would clear more on his own then find his own way out. Clifford at first said that he would feel bad if he left Simon there to finish on his own but Simon said that, "The good Lord would have stopped to help others in their time of need." Clifford retired for the evening and went upstairs to comfort Christine leaving Simon to finish the job.

Christine was awake and desperate to speak to Clifford. He got into bed to comfort her but immediately fell asleep. Christine sat there with her arms folded. "So much for comfort," she said sarcastically.

Back in what was left of the kitchen Simon was busy getting on with his job when unexpectedly a drunken Lydia walked into the dining room with an empty bottle of wine in her hand. She was swaying from side to side with stained mascara down both sides of her cheeks. She threw the empty bottle on the floor and went to grab another full bottle of red wine. Simon jumped up to stop her.

"Stop, Lydia, it's not worth it."

"Oh, don't lecture me, you hardly know anything about me. You're just as bad as my husband. You don't care about Sarah, you're too boring for her."

"I can see you're talking from the bottle," but Simon knew everything she was saying was true.

"No, Simon, I'm telling the true and you know it." Lydia was swaying again so Simon grabbed her, assisting her over to the sofa. Simon told Lydia to stay in the spare bedroom upstairs as Clifford and Christine would not mind. Simon said goodnight then got his coat indicating that he was leaving. Lydia began to cry. "Please, Simon, don't go home and leave me now. I am sorry, I will not say a word."

Simon wanted to leave, but knowing that it would not have been a Catholic thing to do he stayed to keep Lydia company. "Of course I will stay with you for a bit."

Lydia poured Simon a drink. At first he hesitated but then he thought one would not hurt. Lydia poured Simon his ninth glass. They were both as drunk as two alcoholics let loose in a vineyard.

"Do you know?" said Simon slurring his word significantly.

"What is that?" shouted Lydia, laughing for no reason.

"I have never realised how terrifically clever newswipers are."

"News what?" shouted Lydia.

"What new?" said Simon

"You said newswipers, what are newswipers?"

"No, no, no, I said newspapers," Simon corrected her.

"Oh yes, the wallpaper really is something."

"And I thought I was the only person who realised just how lucky we really are to have it," said Simon agreeing, although he was lost and forgot about the mention of newspapers.

"Lydia, I must ask you something."

"Ask away, ask away, the world is your squid."

"Why don't you consider the considerations about considering the Catholic faith membership?"

"Oh no, no, no, I can't take these questions, I can't consider these considerations which you're telling me to consider."

"Why can't you consider?"

"Consider what?"

"I don't know," said Simon.

"What?" questioned Lydia.

"Another drink?" Simon said, offering her the bottle.

"Please," said Lydia, holding up her glass even before Simon had finished his sentence. They chin chinned their glasses and downed the wine. "Yum, that is good stuff," said Lydia licking her lips.

"I couldn't agree more," said Simon. "Do you know, Lydia, I can't imagine why Rufus is not affectionate towards you. You're quite attractive."

"No, stop trying to compliment me, you're lying, it's the drink talking."

"Yes, you're probably right," replied Simon, agreeing that it was the drink talking.

Then she started crying. "Oh, am I really that bad? Does being under the influence of drink make me attractive?"

"Yes... no... I mean..." Simon stopped in his tracks, then he slid off the sofa rolling onto the floor.

"You are a useless human being." Lydia burst into thunderous laugher. Simon did not even hear what Lydia said because he was rolling around on the floor imitating a penguin.

"Do you know any jokes?" asked Lydia randomly.

"Yes, yes, a very good joke as it happens."

"Oh, please do tell?" said Lydia in a posh English accent.

"Okay then, Rufus and Lydia Feldman's marriage. Ha, ha, ha, ha, ha, ha!"

"I don't get it," said Lydia, who was looking completely confused.

"Lydia, you must stop being this unhappy."

"I know, but what can I do, what can I do?"

"Take HRT."

"Do bring my lovely but badly functioning body into this." Lydia shook the bottle. "Simon, we are out of wine."

"There is nothing left," said Simon.

"Now what?" said Lydia, sounding like a lost soul. Lydia and Simon pondered for a while. Once again a planned meal for everyone had ended in disaster. They gazed longingly at each other.

"Simon, could I tempt you?"

"What!" said Simon.

"Do you want me to dance with you? And then we could make passionate love."

Simon pounced on her and suddenly the two of them were laying on the floor making passionate love with Simon forgetting Sarah and his strict Catholic rules, whereas, Lydia thought of Rufus and laughed. Simon was completely lost in this new world outside from the bubble that he had been living in. Lydia knew what was happening but she could not stop herself. They were at it for hours, like sex starved creatures being let loose in a sex shop.

THIRTEEN

The sun rose early next morning. Clifford woke up feeling refreshed and for a minute he had forgotten about his ceiling caving in and the disastrous dinner party. He reached out for his glasses, popped them on his face and went downstairs. The house was a tip. Empty bottles cluttered up the table hiding its beautifully varnished woodwork. Banners, spilt drinks and dirty plates lay on the floor as if a hurricane had entered through the back door. Clifford saw the remains of the mess caused by the episode in the bathroom and groaned. After inspecting his once clean and tidy house Clifford went to open the curtains, and when he did he got the shock of his life. There was Lydia lying naked on top of Simon in the middle of the front garden, but hidden away from the public behind a tall bush. The image was too overwhelming for Clifford to handle and he fainted. After coming round Clifford picked himself up, again saw Lydia and Simon together and fainted for the second time. Eventually Clifford came round again and accepted the image for what it was. He ran towards the front door but as he opened it he saw Rufus getting into his car. Clifford jumped head first out of the door so that Rufus would not spot him and landed in the grass. He did not move an inch as he knew that Rufus would walk over and chat. Clifford watched through the hedge as Rufus drove out of his driveway and disappeared down the road. Clifford crawled to Lydia. He started poking her face and messing up her hair, not that it needed to be messed up, it already was.

"Wake up, Lydia, for heaven's sake, wake up right this minute."

Lydia awoke realising that she was outside in the freezing cold, but was a little surprised to see a fully naked Simon lying under her. "Oh no I forgot that me and Simon were busy last night."

Clifford looked down at the floor. "Oh, Lydia, you slut, how could you do this to Sarah?"

"She doesn't have to know," said Lydia. Then Clifford and Lydia saw Simon open his eye a little.

"Oh, Lydia, when Simon realises the compromising position he is in he is going to have a mental breakdown."

"I'm not so sure about that, it may have done him a favour. I allowed him to open up."

"Excuse me, Lydia, I think you were the one who opened up."

Simon awoke. He began to stretch and yawn. Then his mind was trying to tell him that someone was on him but he was too tired to realise this. Lydia and Clifford were frozen solid, then Clifford let out the slightest little cough.

"Morning, Simon."

"Sarah, what are you doing in my bedroom?" said Simon in an alarming way. "Could you shut the window please, it's freezing in here."

"Err, Simon, it's me, Clifford, and you're outside lying naked in my front garden with Lydia."

Suddenly a playback video formed in Simon's head of him and Lydia snogging passionately on the floor, then making their way into the front garden to re-enact Adam and Eve in the Garden of Eden.

"Oh no," said Simon as it dawned on him that he was outside. Then he realised he was naked. "Oh no." And when he saw a naked Lydia lying in front of him, "Oh! Oh! Oh! Ohhhhh!" Clifford put his hand over Simon's mouth.

"Don't shout, everyone in the street will hear you," but Simon was already in a state of panic.

"Oh what, Simon? You should be thanking your lucky stars. Many men would love to be in your position right now."

"Like who?" said Clifford lost by Lydia's words. "Not even the most desperate virgin in the entire world would rather stay a virgin then be in Simon's position."

"You are a very nasty person, Clifford Cockflint, when you want to be!" snapped Lydia.

Simon jumped up pushing Lydia off him. "Get off me, get off me!" He then started jumping around the garden.

"Oh no, he's getting hysterical," said Clifford.

"Quick, do something," Lydia ordered.

"Like what?" Clifford said.

Simon was going mental, it was like a demon had taken complete control of his body. Suddenly he tripped over a step and fell hard hitting his head on the ground. He was out cold.

Clifford and Lydia hurriedly picked up Simon and carried him inside. Clifford held him by his feet and Lydia carried him by his hands. They laid him on the sofa and Clifford got some water and splashed his face. Simon did not move a muscle.

"Do you think he's dead?" asked Lydia worryingly.

"No but he has knocked himself out. We will just have to wait for him to come round."

While they both waited for Simon to wake up, Lydia started feeling guilty about taking advantage of him and two-timing Rufus. Clifford expressed no sympathy whatsoever. He did not help the situation, in fact he added more to her guilt-ridden thoughts.

"I knew that Rufus made you unhappy, but to ruin his life and now innocent Sarah, I hope you can live with the guilt."

"Yes, thank you, Clifford, I understand what you mean. Just be quiet!" Clifford got a glass of iced water and threw it in Simon's face. He was still unconscious. "Wake up, Simon, I need to go out in a minute." Clifford had booked to take Chris out of the hospital for a few hours. He had planned to take him on an adventure day out to the steam train convention, and the train would take them through the countryside.

Slowly Simon started to come round. He opened his eyes and stared in a complete daze into the eyes of Clifford and Lydia, and then he said, "Hello, Mother."

"Mother?" Lydia said in shock. "Who are you calling 'Mother'?"

"Hello, Father," Simon said to Clifford.

"Don't be ridiculous, Simon. I think you're just a bit traumatised by the whole sleeping with Lydia thing."

"When is school?" asked Simon, in a boyish tone.

"Simon, look, you are a twenty-two year old man, you have a very successful job position," said Clifford trying desperately to remind him of his life. Simon gazed at his surroundings, and a joker-like smile transformed his face.

"I love this house, it's really something. Mummy, why do you look so much older than Daddy?"

Clifford found it difficult not to laugh, but he held his hand over his mouth so Lydia would not see. "Naughty, you naughty boy! Do not show that kind of disrespect towards your mother."

Simon started crying. The tears resembled a child's cry of deep hurt when a mother takes his toy off him for getting into mischief. Clifford clutched tightly onto Lydia to get her attention. "Lydia! What do you think you are doing?"

"I am disciplining our child, you may want him turning into a delinquent imbecile but I for one do not!"

"Earth to Lydia! Earth to Lydia! Simon is a twenty-two year old adult, engaged and has a very successful career. Plus, he is not even our child!"

"Oh yes, of course, how stupid of me."

Clifford and Lydia suddenly jumped from the sound of someone knocking the door.

"What should we do?" asked Lydia, panicking.

"Look out of the window and see who it is?" replied Clifford.

Lydia went over to the window. "Bollocks! It's Sarah!" Lydia shouted. "Unbelievable, this can't be happening."

Clifford and Lydia were bouncing around the room thinking of what to do with Simon. "I know," said Clifford, "we could tell Sarah that Simon had a vision of an angel that told him to change his ways."

"That is the most ridiculous thing I ever heard in my life."

"Have you got a better idea?" Clifford panted. "I'll get the door."

Lydia checked herself in the mirror. She ruffled her hands through her lovely wavy, black hair and tied her clothes up to make herself look more presentable. "Hello, Sarah, how lovely to see you."

"Hi, Lydia, is Simon here?"

"Erm, yes, yes he is as a matter of fact." Lydia's eyes were wide open. She could not have looked any more guilty than what she did right now.

"Are you feeling okay, Lydia, you look ill?"

Lydia froze solid on the spot. Her mouth was open but nothing came out. Sarah waved her hand close up to her face. "Are you okay, Lydia?"

Lydia suddenly came back to Earth. "Oh my word, Sarah, I am so sorry for acting this way. Please forgive me. I think I am still hungover from last night."

Sarah held on to Lydia because she felt that she was unstable. "Grab my arm, Lydia."

Lydia played along. "Thank you, Sarah, I am so glad you turned up."

Before they both went into the living room, Clifford quickly went into the hallway to greet Sarah. "Sarah, how lovely to see you."

"Blimey, I wish I got a greeting like this every day when I come round."

"You do look nice this morning."

"Thank you, Clifford, it's kind of you to say."

"No bother, no bother in the slightest." The three of them stood silently in the hallway, all looking at each other and nodding.

"Well, are we going to go through into the living room or is the place at a standstill?"

"The kitchen is out of bounds but you can go through into the living room." Sarah was about to go in when Clifford suddenly stopped her from entering. "Sarah, stop!" Clifford had never shouted that loud before and Sarah jumped out of her skin. Also Lydia's hair nearly fell out. "Sarah, please forgive me, I did not mean to shout so loud."

"Look, I am not stupid, tell me what is going on. Lydia looks like she has done something like witness a murder, and you, Clifford, seem frightened of something. Did you and Lydia sleep together last night?" Sarah said this intending it to be taken light heartedly. Unfortunately, Clifford and Lydia found this offensive.

"How dare you, Sarah, I am a happily married woman," Lydia snapped in anger.

"Yes, and I would never be unfaithful to Christine," Clifford said in an angry tone.

"I am really sorry, it was just a joke," said Sarah apologetically.

Clifford and Lydia both realised that they had exaggerated for no reason. Then they both laughed hoping that Sarah would not suspect anything.

"Look, this is getting weird, please tell me what is going on otherwise I will call Christine down here to see if she knows."

"No, don't do that please, Sarah," said Clifford. "Christine needs her rest. Last night was a chain of rather unlikely events."

"Okay, but what has happened to Simon?"

Clifford took Sarah's hand. "Sarah, this is quite difficult for me because I know that you are going to find this hard to believe…" Lydia stood there guilt-ridden, nervous and full of admiration, unaware of what Clifford was about to say. Alternatively, she thought, is Clifford going to tell her everything about last night or is he going to create some believable lie to save her neck?

"Last night Simon came upstairs and woke me during the night. He told me that when he was clearing away the left over rubble that was blocking off the kitchen door, a bright mystical glow formed in front of him. This mysterious glow got brighter and brighter, then, as if by magic, the glow started to outline a structure of a body, a female body in time. Simon said that he did not move because he was flabbergasted by this cataclysmic moment. Then an angel appeared. Her feet did not touch the ground, she just hovered above the floor smiling." Clifford was making up this ridiculous story on the spot, and he noticed that Sarah was not following. Her facial expressions gave him the answer that her mind was not processing this information. Lydia refrained from making eye contact with Sarah otherwise her face would have given the story away. "At first," Clifford continued, "I did not believe him. I thought his mind was filled with the devil's drink, alcohol. However, he was not even that drunk, in fact I don't think he was drunk at all."

"Well, Clifford, as you know, Simon never liked to drink anyway."

"Well then, Sarah, in all honesty, how could I make something this extreme up?"

"You're right, Clifford, but look at him. That is not the Simon I remember. He is in his whole world."

Simon sat in the armchair bouncing up and down like a demented child. Clifford leaned into Sarah and whispered softly into her ear, "If you take my advice take advantage of Simon being like this, because when this spell-like mood brushes off it'll be the same

Simon again." Sarah stopped in her tracks. The reality was becoming clearer and clearer. She thought that if Simon really did have a vision from an angel, and he has forgotten what his duties are, then she could control his mind for the next couple of days. A Cheshire cat grin spread across her face. Her mind turned into an out of control computer, and she planned so many things that her and Simon could do for the next few days.

"Oh, Simon, I'm going to look forward to these next few days. Come on, darling, this is Sarah, your girlfriend, I am going to take you home now."

Simon grabbed her hand quickly and he stared at her for a while. "Wow! She is okay, isn't she?" said Simon talking to Clifford. "Excuse, miss, can, can, can, you, you tell me your name, if that is okay with you." Simon was talking like a teenage boy who was about to ask the prettiest girl in the year out.

"Why don't you remember, Simon? It's me, Sarah."

"Sarah, you don't look like a Sarah."

"Really? What would you think my name is then?"

"I thought you were going to introduce yourself as Summer, but not a Sarah."

"Summer, I don't look like a Summer," said Sarah.

"Actually you do look like a Summer," Clifford said, agreeing with Simon.

"Simon, would you like to come back to our house now?"

"Wow, you mean we live in a house together?"

"Yes, we have lived there now for just over a year."

"I want to see it." Simon dived off the sofa quicker than a squirrel jumping on his nuts.

"Wait for me, Simon, I've got the house keys." The door slammed behind Sarah as she walked out. Clifford wiped his brow with his sleeve glad that Sarah bought his lie and suspected nothing. Lydia was relieved too. "We must never talk about this again," said Clifford.

"I absolutely agree." Before they both went their separate ways Lydia turned to Clifford looking more serious than she had looked in her life. "Oh my word, what is the matter, Lydia?" said Clifford worryingly. "You know how desperate Sarah is for Simon's love."

"Yes," Lydia replied.

"Well, when Simon finally makes love to her... she is going to be so disappointed. He is crap at sex!"

FOURTEEN

Chris stared in amazement at the town which Clifford drove him through. Because Chris had been in the hospital for so long, he had almost forgotten what a town looked like. Clifford knew that all he needed was a break from the hospital and a bit of fresh air.

"Now, Chris, I have wanted to take you to this library for a while. I have a feeling that you are going to love it, or I could take you through the countryside, but I cannot take you to the steam train convention as it does not open till next month. Funnily enough it is actually the day after Rufus and Lydia's wedding anniversary."

"Let's go to the library, I like the sound of that."

"No problem," said Clifford. He was secretly relieved that Chris chose the library. "It's a great place with more than twenty-eight thousand books to choose from."

"I could never read that amount of books."

"Ha, you should meet the wacky librarian, Mr Fickwick, I think he has read all the books and is now bouncing from wall to wall in that magnificent building he spends so much of his life in."

"He sounds different," said Chris. "My perception of a librarian differs from your reality, Clifford. I thought librarians were quiet, sometimes grumpy and rude."

"Crikey, Chris, Mr Fickwick is a very proud librarian. Eccentric is the right word."

"He won't come close to my face will he?" said Chris who utterly despised people talking only inches away from his face.

"No, you will be all right, it's just a figure of speech. Mr Fickwick is as harmless as a butterfly but he can sometimes be very full on."

"Full on what?" said Chris confused.

"Not literally 'full on' but Mr Fickwick can sometimes get very excited about a newbie entering his library. Everybody knows him you see and he knows what everybody's favourite genre is, and he loves guessing what the public want to read."

"Wow, he sounds psychic," said Chris, who was impressed by the sound of this man.

"I would not test his skill, he knows what to do about anything, he is a very independent person who relies on no one."

"Has he worked at the library for a long time?" Chris enquired.

"That is a good question. Let me think now, Mr Fickwick turned fifty-six the other day, he started working there when he was twenty-nine just after he gave up being a professor of English literature, so that is twenty-seven years he has been at the library."

"He was a professor?"

"Yes he was, and a very young professor too, but he knew that his passion was within the four walls of the town library so he gave up his job and started working there, and he has been there ever since."

Clifford turned at the traffic lights into the road in which the library was on. It was busy as it was a Saturday.

"This place is busy," said Chris, looking at everyone who was out and about. "I wish my parents would have taken me to places like this."

"Why don't they?" asked Clifford.

"My parents do not understand how people with Asperger's works. They think that I am going to behave in an embarrassing way."

"Oh, Chris, I am sure that is not true."

"It really is, Clifford, they would understand me so much better if they spent time with me, but no, I get ratty in a classroom one time and they think it best if they lock me up in a building and then just forget about me."

"Would you like me to talk to them?"

"No, forget it. Honestly, if I did not see them again it would not bother me in the slightest."

"Don't say that, Chris."

"No, Clifford, I am being serious. Where are they? If I had not been introduced to you then I would still be stuck in my room back at the hospital."

"Are your parents uneducated?" asked Clifford. He did not want to get into the personalities of his parents but since Chris had started Clifford was not going to back down.

"Oh yes, they are very educated people. My dad came from London, he grew up in a house that had servants, and my mum also came from London, she too grew up around money. My parents were not loved emotionally by their parents, but they were given possessions. They are two very confused and unloving people."

Clifford listened intently.

"My parents were delighted when they bought their new house together. It was everything they were used too. Big expensive rooms filled with everything that a person could wish for. Then eventually my mum gave birth to me and I was more or less brought up by the servants. When I was younger the servants noticed that I was acting differently, and some of the teachers when I was in the infants mentioned to them that I was different from the other children. My parents would explode. They would tell the servant who reported it to them that the teacher was not doing her job right. Then they would give that servant a written warning because he or she believed that teacher."

Chris stared out of the window as he was telling Clifford his memories. Clifford listened taking in every word Chris was saying. "How long was it till your parents found out about your Asperger's?" Clifford asked.

"When I was fourteen. One morning my parents burst into school as they were fed up of teachers saying things. They were concerned about their reputation. And so eventually they were told that I had Asperger's syndrome. Seven hours later they admitted me to the psychiatric hospital."

Clifford's jaw dropped.

"I remember coming home that evening to find my wardrobe had been emptied, but at that stage I wasn't too bothered. I thought my room was being redecorated and then my parents said we are going for a little drive." Chris paused remembering. He was holding back his tears. "And then my parents kissed me goodbye and I watched them drive away leaving me in the hands of strangers." Chris's voice sounded strained as he did not want to cry. "I thought that eventually they would come back. In the past three years they have only visited me six times, each visit lasting no longer than forty-five minutes."

"Chris I want to help you through this, you have so much potential. We can show people, including your parents, what you can achieve." Just as Clifford was about to continue someone banged loudly on the window of his car. Clifford and Chris almost jumped out of their skin.

"Wow, it's you, it's you, Mr Clifford Cockflint, the man who was involved in that great accident."

"Yes, it is me," said Clifford, winding down his window.

"This is indeed a pleasure," said the builder. He touched Clifford's skin and his eyes widened. "Wow, you're real!"

"I am glad you found my small adventure exciting. And yes, I am real," laughed Clifford.

"I bet your life has been very quiet since your adventure."

Clifford had to refrain from laughing, and he spoke to the worker quickly then parked his car and took Chris inside the library to meet Mr Fickwick, the most famous librarian within the United Kingdom.

Chris was bewildered by the appearance of the library. It looked bigger than and looked similar to the Taj Mahal. Clifford and Chris walked up the stairs and saw Mr Fickwick sticking up posters of books old and new on the wall. As you walk into the library there are pictures of Mr Fickwick with different authors hanging on the wall. Chris noticed that the librarian had the stereotypical professor appearance. He had wild white hair that could do with a haircut or maybe just a comb, and glasses which hung at the end of his nose. He had a vintage dress look with a tweed jacket with a colourful shirt, and bow tie with chequered trousers. He wore slippers instead of shoes because he was at the library all day and he found them more comfortable. Mr Fickwick was talking to some customers and his arms were flailing all over the place. Clifford knew that when he was acting like that he was reciting some scene from a book. The customers simply adored Mr Fickwick, he was a genuine, kind person and highly respected by the public. As Mr Fickwick was talking he noticed Clifford and Chris standing by the entrance. He loved it when Clifford came in so he waved to acknowledge them both. On the wall in big letters it says 'Silence If You Please'. Mr Fickwick put that sign up on the wall but always broke his own rule as he shouted across the silent area. "Ah, hooray, my very good friend Clifford has just walked in. What an honour it is to be in his presence. I'll be over in a minute, I'm just telling these charming people about the time my great, great uncle told Shakespeare that he needed a haircut."

Clifford started laughing. The people were amazed how quickly it slipped Mr Fickwick's mind that they were in a library, in particular the silent area. Some people laughed to themselves, however, there was always one coffin dodger who objected.

"How can I read the newspaper properly with that great oaf shouting?" Mr Fickwick being Mr Fickwick took no notice. 'Be happy' was his motto.

"Oh, what is there to be happy about?" snapped the old coffin dodger.

"Be happy!" bellowed Mr Fickwick. He was not being sarcastic or purposely trying to irritate the old coffin dodger. He really meant it.

"Why does he shout so loud?" asked Chris.

"It's simply because that is the way he is. Loud and jolly are the two best words to describe him. Honestly, Chris," Clifford continued, "Mr Fickwick is that loud he could be heard in silent films."

"I could never be that loud," said Chris.

"You just need more confidence, young Chris," said Clifford kindly.

Mr Fickwick said goodbye to the couple he was speaking to, then he marched over to Clifford and grabbed his hand.

"Splendid to see you, Clifford, absolutely splendid, it is always a pleasure, my good old friend."

"And of course it is nice to see you, Mr Fickwick."

"Very kind, too kind, Clifford, I am not worthy of your kind words. You'll have to forgive that customer over there, she tends to be a little cranky."

"Really?" said Clifford jokingly.

"Honestly, Clifford," said Mr Fickwick, and he turned him around to whisper in his ear. "Between you and me, she sleeps with a dildo the size of a shotgun." Clifford tried not to laugh as the old coffin dodger looked over.

"How is that gorgeous wife of yours?" enquired Mr Fickwick.

"Christine's okay, she has had better days, but fine nonetheless."

"That is super to hear," said Mr Fickwick, running his hands through his wild, willow-like hair and making it messier. "How have you been since the accident?" he asked.

"I'm okay now," said Clifford. "Christine and I have moved on from that catastrophe and on to the next one."

"Oh dilly dally dear," said Mr Fickwick. "What is the trouble now, kind Clifford."

"Our bathroom ceiling caved in last night and now Christine is not in a good way. That is why I said she has had better days. The builders are there now sorting it out, but it's still a hassle."

"No, no, no, nothing is a hassle, Clifford. Remember that, my friend. However, you have come to the right place if you need to cheer yourself up. Now what book should I suggest for you today? Now let me think about this carefully." Mr Fickwick stood there scratching his head. "Think, brain, think."

"Well actually, Mr Fickwick," interrupted Clifford, I have my friend here with me now. His name is Chris and he loves reading."

Mr Fickwick quicker than a flash grabbed Chris in delight. "Welcome to the library, young man, I am always delighted to welcome a new guest to this magnificent library. Now you have made the first and best step of entering this place, and now the fun part which is exploring this building from top to bottom." Mr Fickwick was jumping in the air and waving his arms around. He looked as if he had taken a serious dosage of speed. "Now, what do you like reading? Oh no, no, no, no, no, don't tell me, I have a wonderful talent of knowing what people like to read just by studying their faces. Now it's autobiographies for you, my boy. We have the latest from Paul Merton to David Jason to Susan Boyle, I would ask her to sing here but she would sing too loud in the silent area. No, no, no! Wait, you read horror. Oh yes, I see it now, how stupid of me to think that you were an autobiography person. It's Stephen King all the way for you. We have them all, *The Shining* being my favourite. Forget the film though, ah please do forget the film, do not even waste your valuable time. No, wait, you're a fantasy book fan, you like adventures about the heroic and legendary

King Arthur along with the brilliant master of all magical mystery, Merlin the mighty wizard."

Clifford could see that Chris felt overwhelmed by Mr Fickwick, but he found it difficult to interrupt him as he knew when he gets talking there is no stopping him.

"You want a good laugh? Please, please, please, I urge you to read *The Wind in the Willows* and get familiar with the classic fictional characters of Mole, Rat, Toad and Badger. Oh my goodness, the Toad is an unforgettable character he truly is. The world has held great heroes as history books have showed, but never someone like Toad."

Finally Clifford was able to interrupt him. "Chris, will you be okay to venture around the building and I'll catch up with you in a minute?"

Chris quite happily went off by myself.

"Mr Fickwick, you did not let me explain. You need to go easy with Chris, he has Asperger's syndrome."

"I have cream for that," replied Mr Fickwick.

"What are you talking about?" said Clifford aghast.

"Spots are a terrible thing for people of his age. Mind you, his face did not look that bad to me."

"Mr Fickwick, Asperger's syndrome is a type of autism."

"Oh, how stupid of me. Yes, I remember now, I read a fantastic book called *The Curious Incident of the Dog in the Night-Time.*"

"Yes, so go easy on Chris. I am trying to help him build on his confidence. Chris has a lot of problems within his home life. Basically his parents do not understand the concept of what Asperger's really is, therefore they have put him in a hospital and he has not had any communication with the outside world for a long time."

Mr Fickwick paused. Things like this upset him. He turned and watched Chris wander up and down the aisles looking attentively at the books. "Clifford, honestly, leave it with me, I know what to do. What kind of books does he read? Crikey, I am actually asking someone what they like to read. I need to retire."

Clifford laughed. "He reads adventure stories."

"Right, I know exactly what to do."

Meanwhile, just down the road from the library was the river. Sarah had hired out a rowing boat for the day with Simon rowing for her. The river was not too busy and Sarah felt that they were having a great time, bonding more.

"This is nice, isn't it?" said Sarah.

"It most certainly is," said Simon. "We must do this more often."

"Really?" shouted Sarah in surprise. "You want us to do this more often?"

"Yes, why not? I mean how long have we been together now?" said Simon, who was still confused about being in a relationship in the first place.

"We have been together for four years and been engaged for a year."

"Oh yes, that's right, Samantha."

"It's Sarah."

"Why did you never introduce me to this place?"

"Because you were working, and then you get in from work and then go off to your presentation evenings to speak about the Catholic faith."

"Wait, wait, wait. I'm a Catholic?"

"Yes. Oh, surely you must remember that. An angel spoke to you last night." Just then Sarah saw three boats with the people in them staring at her as if she was mad.

"Keep rowing that way please, Simon," said Sarah, pointing straight on to get away from the other rowers.

"What angel? Have you been sniffing something naughty, Sarah?"

"No I haven't. Never mind, the angel obviously wiped your memory from last night."

"Okay, Sarah."

Simon looked at Sarah as if she had three heads. He could still not remember anything from last night and his moment with Lydia had been completely erased from his mind – for now anyway. Simon continued to row. They were having a great time on the river and Sarah had never been so happy at the prospect of spending time with Simon. The weather was good and the sun was gleaming brightly, reflecting off the water. The oars dipped softly in and out of the water and both Simon and Sarah were enjoying the peace and quiet. Couples of all ages were pacing up and down either side of the lake enjoying each other's company, while professional rowers glided by.

"Are you looking forward to the wedding?" Sarah asked randomly.

"Are we getting married?" said Simon, who shot his head up so quick that he almost got whiplash.

"Yes, Simon, we are. How many more times do I have to tell you? We are getting married in about three months' time."

"Oh yes, I remember now," Simon agreed, although he was lying. He could not remember anything about planning a wedding or even asking Sarah to marry him.

"It's going to be great, Simon, we have nearly made it to the big day having bought everything in time."

"Are there many more days that are important that I ought to know?"

"Well, next week it's Rufus and Lydia's thirtieth wedding anniversary."

"Who are they?" said Simon, who genuinely could not remember who Rufus and Lydia were.

"Oh my goodness, Simon, can you really not remember who they are?"

"No I can't. Why, are they important people?"

"Well, they are important to me."

"Are they a happy couple?"

"Well, I am not sure that they are always happy, but they try their best, although Rufus can be thoughtless sometimes."

"He must have something that is bugging him."

"I'm not so sure about that. They now have nothing in common, they don't communicate with each other, they have never had children and they don't have sex. Actually, they are a typical British couple," laughed Sarah.

"Are we intimate?" asked Simon. Sarah was struck by this question and she was unsure how to answer it, so she tried to think of how to make him want to love her before the wedding.

"Normally we have sex on Tuesdays, Thursdays and Sundays, sometimes Mondays if the weather's good."

"Oh really, we have sex that much?" Simon suddenly realised that the day was Tuesday. "So later we will have sex together?"

"Yes we will," said Sarah happily.

Simon could not wait to make love to Sarah. He was so desperate to get her home, then he remembered that they had a picnic earlier. The basket was behind Sarah and inside the basket was a thick picnic blanket. He felt nervous about asking Sarah a rather awkward question.

"Erm, Sarah, can I ask you a question?"

"Sure," she replied.

"Do you think it would be romantic if we had sex now, right here on this little boat, with just the blanket to cover us."

"I'm not too sure about that, even though there is no one about and no one to disturb us." Sarah was getting to the point of saying a thousand yeses. "Okay then, I don't see why not." Sarah could not wait to start lovemaking with Simon, and she did not care if they were on a boat or not. She stood up to sit on his lap and kissed him passionately. She sat on his lap and for a while they were just kissing. Due to neither Simon nor Sarah controlling the rowing boat, it started drifting off on its own. There were two ways the boat could have gone. Boats were restricted from going into the left lane as it was known for dangerous rapids. Unfortunately the boat did indeed enter the rapids but Simon and Sarah were completely oblivious to this. They were really getting things going when the boat hit the first wave and then Sarah, as if she was as light as a feather, was thrown overboard. Simon held on to the sides of the boat and shouted her name.

"Sarah, my love, where are you?" Sarah's head bobbed above the water but the waves ran over her. Eventually the waves pushed her to the water's edge. Sarah got up with grass hanging from her hair. She was drenched but she quickly ran down the pathway calling out Simon's name who was still sitting on the boat fearing for his life.

"Simon, try and control the boat!" shouted Sarah. Simon could not hear her and by now the boat was taking on water.

"Oh no!" shouted Simon panicking. He got down on his knees and tried as hard as he could to splash the water off the boat and back into the lake. Water continued to pour into the boat until the it could not hold any more and the boat started sinking. After ten seconds the boat was lost under the lake never to be seen again. Simon splashed his way to the shore and Sarah stuck her hand out for Simon to reach.

"Simon, grab my hand." Simon grabbed Sarah's hand and she pulled him to the shore. They were both drenched and tired and they held hands and walked wearily home.

Chris sat quietly at one of many tables that were in the library. He picked a few books to flick through, and Clifford went to wander round the aisles himself. As he wandered up and down the aisles he hoped that one day he would have published a book and it would have its own permanent space at this library. Clifford then saw Rufus in search of a book. "Hi, Rufus, what are you doing here?"

"I am getting a book for my friend's birthday."

"Then why are you in a library?"

"Clifford, what a silly question, I want to get them a book."

"No, what I mean is you cannot buy a book from a library, you can only borrow."

"Crikey, Clifford, I am not that stupid, I'm borrowing a book for them to read. There is no way I am paying £11.99 for a book. It's not worth the expense."

"But, Rufus, what if they enjoy the book?"

"Well, they can always renew it."

Rufus said nothing more for a short while and that surprised Clifford.

"How is the kitchen coming along?" Rufus then enquired.

"It's coming along good. Christine rang me not so long ago."

"How is Christine?"

"She is okay considering what you caused."

"Look, Clifford, I said I was sorry."

"Okay, okay, I'm sorry. I should not go on." Clifford then remembered about Lydia spending the night with Simon. "Oh, err, Rufus, have you seen Lydia today?"

"No, I have not seen her today. Hopefully she will be home when I get there. I need to tell her that I got her adopted brother a library book for his birthday." Clifford laughed quietly to himself. "Why are you here then?" asked Rufus.

"I have taken Chris out for the day. I feel that this place will give him some confidence."

"Introduce me please."

"No," Clifford said bluntly, "I said I want him to build his confidence up, not have what little he has left destroyed."

"Clifford, you make me sound like a horrible person."

"Well the way you are towards Lydia you are."

"That's different, Lydia is my wife."

"Oh, Rufus, you do talk such rubbish," said Clifford, switching himself off so he would not have to endure any more of Rufus's ridiculous comments.

Mr Fickwick then walked around the corner. "Well, Mr Fickwick, have you thought of a way to help Chris build his confidence up?"

"Yes indeed, young Clifford, the next time you take Chris out from the hospital ring me up in advance and I'll invite some people to the library, but don't worry it's all for a good cause. A 'Fickwick idea' if you please."

Clifford never felt worried by Mr Fickwick's ideas because he knew that it would always turn out to be for the best.

"Good afternoon, Rufus, what brings you to the library?"

"Oh, I'm just getting your birthday present."

"Oh lovely, tell my adopted sister I said hello." Mr Fickwick was Lydia's older brother. They were not close but close enough. Mr Fickwick spends too much time in the library for him to visit Clifford, Christine and the gang. He is married to his work and he sacrificed having a wife and children because he knew he would not be able to put his marriage and children first. Getting older and being alone did not faze him either. He had so much planned if he could face the idea of retirement. It was a long way off but as Mr Fickwick says, "Time flies when you're having fun."

FIFTEEN

Christine was resting in the front room watching television. She had cancelled all her appointments for the week, and she was contemplating cancelling her next week's appointments too. As she sat drinking her tea Christine continued to dwell on what her life would be like if she moved house to be closer to her children. Clifford and Christine had one girl and one boy. The girl Michelle had emigrated to Australia for work purposes. She had told her parents that she would work out there for three years and then return to work in London. However, she met and instantly fell in love with an Australian musician, therefore Michelle decided to stay in Australia. She travelled to visit her mother when she had cancer, but she has not seen her since she got the all-clear. Christine loves the fact that she rings every day but it's not the same as talking to her face to face. Also Clifford and Christine's son Malcolm moved abroad to teach in New York, then travelled to the most exotic and challenging places in the world like the Amazon jungle. He wrote about his adventures in a book and, like his father, Malcolm had a passion to write. Malcolm had always been very close to his parents, so when he decided to flee the nest Clifford and Christine went through the pain of saying goodbye to another child. Malcolm also rings home every day but Christine craved to be with them.

"Christine, I am home!" Clifford shouted as he came into the house.

"I'm in the front room, darling," Christine replied.

"Oh, I see the builders have done a lot today." Clifford glanced at the new ceiling in the kitchen.

"They arrived just as you left this morning."

Clifford thought back to the morning and remembered that Lydia and Simon had spent the night together. Simon accidently fell and knocked himself out cold causing him to lose his memory. Then he tricked Sarah into believing that Simon had had a vision from an angel from heaven, and she believed it.

"What did you do this morning?" asked Christine.

"I cannot remember," Clifford lied.

"I have not seen Lydia all day. I thought that she might pop round."

"I don't think so," said Clifford.

"Why not?"

"Well, you know, she might feel partly guilty about the whole caving in ceiling scenario."

"Why should she feel guilty? After all, it was her idiotic husband's fault."

Clifford knew by the tone of her voice that something was wrong, she sounded more ratty and irritable then she had in a long while. He went up to her and sat down.

"Christine, are you okay because you don't sound okay? You seem very irritated about something. Look, if it's about last night I assured you that it will all be fixed and put right."

"Clifford, you are not going to like this because we have had this discussion before, but I am considering giving up my job and moving to New York to be with Malcolm, and then I won't be as far from Michelle as I am here. What do you say?"

Clifford had never enjoyed travelling. In fact when Christine used to announce that they were going on holiday the next year, the plane journey would be on his mind every single day. He would suffer terrible and very traumatic nightmares which would distress him. In the end Christine agreed that she would not put him through that again. However, when their children moved away Christine missed them far too much. She needed them.

"Christine, I think about Michelle and Malcolm every day, not a minute goes by when they do not enter my mind, but I simply cannot do it, love. I cannot leave England and move to New York. It's not my place."

"But I need to be with my children. I cannot bear another birthday without them. Another Christmas without them. Another absent Mother's Day meal without them. I need my children." Christine suddenly sounded very desperate, and a sense of sheer pain was leaping off every word she spoke.

"Christine, where has this sudden outburst come from?"

"It has come out of nowhere. I miss them. It does not matter how many hours I work, how much money I make, where we go or what we do, that still does not make up for the time I am not spending with the children."

"Look, I have a compromise for you. Why don't you go to New York for two weeks, stay with Malcolm for a bit then, later on in the year, you can go to spend time with Michelle out in Australia?"

"You just said two things that will not work in my defence. One, you are not with me, and secondly a holiday for me to go to New York then later in the year go to Australia is impossible financially. My cancer last year raised my insurance up too high and we cannot afford it. That is why I want to move out there."

"I am sorry, Christine, but I have all my responsibilities here, plus moving to New York would be the last thing I would want to do."

"Do it for your children then, Clifford."

"Please don't put me in that position. Actually, have you even told Malcolm that you plan to move near him?"

"How could I say anything? I needed to know what you want."

"And now that you know what is your plan?"

"I don't know, I really don't know."

"Well, I'll let you sleep on it, then we can talk about it tomorrow maybe."

Clifford went to the unmarked bit of the kitchen and started to organise dinner. Christine got up and looked at their family pictures. She was missing her children more now than she ever had.

Late in the evening Rufus and Lydia were sitting at their dinner table, but a flowing conversation was absent from it. Rufus felt guilty about being the cause of the Cockflint's kitchen ceiling caving in and upsetting Christine, whereas Lydia felt guilty for being unfaithful towards Rufus. She was quite surprised just how guilty she felt, but underneath it all she knew that Rufus was her husband and he was the first person she had fallen in love with. Every time she was about to break the ice she stopped herself and said nothing at all. Rufus found it difficult to say nothing and eventually broke the silence. "Lydia, I was watching this drama, a murder mystery programme, and it was so depressing. The woman constantly cheated on her husband."

Lydia started choking. She thought that he was implying something. She snapped once again. "Why are you telling me about someone who is being unfaithful? I wouldn't be unfaithful. Are you calling me an unfaithful wife?" Lydia was panicking, and Rufus was taken aback at how she was reacting.

"Lydia, I was not implying anything, I simply just wanted to chat to you about anything." Rufus felt drained from all the arguments, disagreements and shouted aggressive words.

"Oh, I see, I'm sorry. So what did you say the name of the show was?" said Lydia, trying to make Rufus not suspect anything if she hurriedly changed the subject.

"I'm am not sure. I think it was a murder mystery. There were loads of people crying and two deaths, it was really depressing."

"Oh, I know. It's called *EastEnders*."

"That is not a murder mystery."

"No, but everything you just described there happens in *EastEnders*."

Then the room went back to silence but it was not a good silence. Rufus and Lydia were sitting face to face at the table and quite close together, and Rufus felt that it was him that was making her feel uncomfortable. He knew that the next week was their thirtieth wedding anniversary and he wanted to buy her something special. Lydia was unsure whether or not they would make it. Then Rufus thought of something to start a conversation. His head shot up.

"Lydia, you won't believe this but I saw Simon and Sarah together and he looked like he was on another planet."

"Why would I want to know about that? What has Simon's and Sarah's business to do with me? I don't care!" Lydia snapped harshly.

"For heaven's sake, Lydia, why does everything I say have to end in an argument? I am sick to death of you getting angry every time I say something. You are very good friends with Sarah and you're always saying that Simon mistreats her, and now that I have seen them together you come out with rubbish and start being defensive. Has Simon or Sarah said anything to you?"

Lydia realised that she was acting in a strange way, therefore she took a deep breath and said in a calm voice, "Oh darling, I am sorry, I must be very tired." Then she said something that completely astonished Rufus. "Why don't we have an early night."

Now Rufus almost choked. "Really? What, right now?"

"Well I don't see why not," said Lydia.

"Blimey," said Rufus. "Normally you don't get dessert if you have not finished your dinner."

Five minutes later...

They both came downstairs. "Well, look at that," said Lydia. "At least the dinner is still warm."

Later in the evening Rufus was in his study marking school books and Lydia just lounged on the sofa in her front room. She watched television but did not take a lot in. She then thought to herself, I hope the rest of my life is not going to be like this. Rufus was still in his study and he decided to have a break. He did something that he had never done before. He decided to wander around his room and look at the books that were on his shelves.

"And then Simon took me out for the most romantic meal we have ever been on. How about that then?" Sarah's verbal diarrhoea was pouring out of her as she sat on Christine's sofa telling her about her day with Simon.

"I'm really pleased for you but I don't understand his sudden change."

"I know, isn't it amazing. I will always thank that angel that managed to communicate with him. Oh, there is a God." Sarah almost became delirious.

"What are you talking about, Sarah? What angel?" Christine was lost and felt discombobulated.

"Christine, I don't know why you're acting so surprised. After all, I'm surprised Clifford did not tell you about it, he told me in front of Lydia this morning."

"I didn't even know Lydia and Simon were here this morning. Did they stay the night?" Christine enquired.

"It all seemed very suspicious this morning. Clifford and Lydia were acting very peculiar around each other. It almost seemed as if they did something that they were guilty of."

All of a sudden and without warning Christine got a nervous feeling in her stomach and she felt sick.

"Are you all right, Christine? It looks as if you have seen a ghost."

"No, no, I'm fine, I'm okay. I just had a thought, but I hate myself for even contemplating it."

"Why, what were you thinking?"

"No, it's fine, just forget it." Christine appeared to be uncomfortable as she began to fidget.

"Christine, you're going to laugh when I tell you this, but it looked as if Clifford and Lydia were having a secret love affair." Christine spat out her tea and her cup fell to the floor. Sarah panicked and started slapping her back with force. "Oh, Christine, I apologise unreservedly for that joke, it was purely just a joke."

"No, Sarah, I don't think it was a joke because that is what I just thought," said Christine, coughing to get all the tea out of her throat.

"Oh, no, no, Christine, I was only joking about that. Like Clifford would see another woman, and Lydia of all people. It's impossible."

"Everything you have just said to me is complete claptrap. I have never heard such a ridiculous story in my life, and I have read some of Clifford's students' work and believe me that takes some beating."

"Oh no, stop talking like that, Christine."

"No, Sarah. Can you honestly say you believe that Simon had a vision from an angel, because I don't believe that story."

"Well, there is only one way to end this debate, Christine."

"How?"

"Let's ask Clifford," said Sarah.

Christine went upstairs to get Clifford who was speaking to Chris on the phone. Normally Christine would not interrupt Clifford when he was on the phone because she hated being disturbed when she was talking, but in this case she felt it was an emergency.

"Really, Chris, I am so pleased for you, and you're getting on with Mr Fickwick okay? He is not getting too much for you?" Clifford made time for Chris whenever he rang. Christine hammered her fist on the bedroom door and Clifford almost jumped out of his skin. "Sorry, Chris, can I ring you back? Something is happening. Speak to you soon." Clifford slammed the phone down and ran to the door and saw Christine standing there with a face as red as a tomato and a tea stain on her skirt. "Oh my goodness, Christine, what is the matter? Are you okay?"

"Please, Clifford, would you come down for a moment?"

Clifford was worried and walked down the stairs with Christine. "Is your health okay?" said Clifford. Christine refrained from speaking as they both entered the front room. Clifford saw Sarah sitting with a concerned look on her face. Clifford was an intelligent person and it was apparent to him that she knew something. He remained standing whereas Christine sat down in her armchair.

"Now, Clifford, I need you to be honest with me."

"Okay," said Clifford. He felt his head, back and stomach begin to sweat, and his hands were trembling.

"What is the matter, Clifford, why are you shaking?" said Christine who was becoming more and more suspicious by her husband's behaviour.

"Look, Christine, this unexpected confrontation is unfair."

"What confrontation?" said Christine.

"Okay, just ask me what you want to know?" said Clifford, looking at the clock. He could hear it ticking slowly and loudly.

"Clifford, why was Lydia here so early this morning? She did not say anything about staying overnight, plus she left before Rufus left."

"What are you insinuating?" said Clifford.

"Are you and Lydia having an affair, and did Simon catch you in the act?" said Christine bluntly.

Clifford was gobsmacked by his wife's accusation and actually felt insulted by her distrust towards him. Just as Clifford was about to answer her Lydia barged in. "Evening all, I thought I would come in as the door was unlocked."

Lydia felt the tension in the room grab her by the throat. "Have I called at a bad time?" No one answered her. "Okay, I'll come back later."

Christine found her voice. "No, Lydia, hold it right there." Lydia froze but did not move back into the front room immediately.

"Do I have to come in? I've changed my mind, I need to go home."

"No, no, Mrs Feldman, you're not getting away so quickly," said Christine. "We need a chat."

Clifford felt that his interrogation was very unfair and he was angry with Christine and Sarah.

"Now wait a minute, Christine. These questions are very unfair and I'm beginning to lose my patience. Now tell me what exactly are you trying to say?"

"Are you having an affair with Lydia?" Clifford and Lydia stared at each other then suddenly Clifford could not control himself and he started laughing, but once he started laughing he could not stop himself.

"Clifford, why are you laughing?" asked Christine.

"I am laughing at you, Christine."

Christine was taken aback by Clifford's behaviour.

"I cannot believe that you would think that I would have an affair with Lydia. Honestly, Lydia of all people."

"Excuse me, Clifford, why do you always talk about me in that horrible fashion?" snapped Lydia.

Christine sat next to Sarah worried that she had actually had to ask her husband something that she thought she would never have to ask. That hurt her deeply but she still pushed for answers about the morning after the ceiling caved in.

"Listen, Clifford, what were you and Lydia doing this morning?"

"We were talking to Simon," said Clifford.

"About what?" shouted Christine. "I really don't understand what is going on!"

"There is nothing to discuss, Christine," said Clifford.

"Listen, Christine," said Lydia, "I would never hurt you in that way. I have too much respect for you."

"No, no, you two are not getting away this easy. Something is going on," said Christine.

Lydia was about to come clean about everything when Sarah's mobile phone rang. She chose to answer it rather than ignore it. "Sorry, everyone, Simon has cooked dinner for me." Sarah quickly left, and it was almost as if she had forgotten about the conversation about the suspicion of an affair between Clifford and Lydia. The minute Sarah left Clifford grabbed Christine and sat her down.

"Look, Christine, why did you keep badgering Lydia and I when we were trying to protect Sarah."

"Why would you be protecting Sarah?" asked Christine.

Clifford looked up at Lydia. His face spelt out to her that it was time they both told Christine the truth about the long night of the disastrous dinner party.

SIXTEEN

It was early afternoon, the sun was shining brightly and once again the public were out walking around the town and the river was occupied by rowers. People were walking in and out of the library. New York is known as the city that never sleeps, Mr Fickwick's library is known as the library that never stops. Clifford sat at the computer planning to write a book, and as he sat there he contemplated all the different subjects he could tackle. He got very frustrated because he knew there was a book in him but he could never get it down on paper. As he was getting irritated with himself he sat back to admire his surroundings, but Clifford was extremely proud of how confident Chris had become thanks to Mr Fickwick's idea. Mr Fickwick came up with the idea of giving Chris his own session, so that if people wanted to read one of the books that Chris had already read they could ask Chris what it was about. After a couple of days people asked Chris questions about other books and this was giving him a new lease of life. Mr Fickwick was wandering around the aisles like he normally did when he saw Clifford sitting at the computer, staring. Mr Fickwick went over to him.

"Are you okay, young Clifford?" he enquired.

"I'm okay, Mr Fickwick, but I would love to be able to write something good that people would read, remember and maybe like." Mr Fickwick looked at the computer screen and all that Clifford had written was his name at the top of the page. "Oh, Mr Fickwick, I think I am going to be one of those failed writers."

Mr Fickwick absolutely despised anyone who put themselves down and what Clifford was saying angered him. "What are you talking about? You are Clifford Cockflint, the man who has experienced weird and surreal adventures. Write about your accidents, man, turn them into adventure stories and then maybe you could base your assistant on Chris. Refer back to your relationship with Christine, you two have had such an interesting life. Don't leave anything out, write it all down, make the sad bits funny or be completely honest. Create characters but put your lives in those characters. After all these years of reading, it's the authors with the most interesting lives who write books that turn out to be bestsellers."

"That is a brilliant idea, Mr Fickwick," said Clifford. "Well, it's definitely a start."

"Cliff, do you remember my publishing years?"

"Yes, why?" asked Clifford.

"Well why don't you allow me to be your writing agent? I know the best people in the publishing business. Just imagine it, Clifford." Mr Fickwick put his arm around Clifford and helped him imagine his book in the public eye the next year.

"Picture it, Clifford, you publish your book, I help you with every aspect of it, the font, the size, the structure and even help you design the cover of it. Then every day for the first month here in the library I can organise book signings for you. It's a perfect match."

"Mr Fickwick, you have got yourself a deal!" Clifford was so pleased with Mr Fickwick's advice and Mr Fickwick could see he had opened a door within Clifford. "Just consider this please, Mr Fickwick. What if you read the book and it is utter drivel, unreadable, terrible, unpublishable."

"Silence, dear boy," Mr Fickwick raised his hand indicating Clifford to stop talking.

"Yes?" said Clifford.

"I am your agent and I have years of experience. Trust me, if I thought something you wrote was rubbish then I would tell you. I would not just let you write paragraph upon paragraph and just say, oh yes they are fine. Oh no, no, no, that is not how I work."

"That is a relief to hear, Mr Fickwick, I do like honesty."

"Clifford, stop worrying otherwise your creative juices will not be able to flow. You have the potential, Clifford, and I am here to help, not interfere."

"Where do you find the time for all this?" asked Clifford.

"I find and make time," said Mr Fickwick, rubbing his hands like a villain.

"Mr Fickwick, you're crazy. I fail to understand why you never advertise a job vacancy."

"Now, now, Clifford," said Mr Fickwick, "you know I hate that phrase 'advertise a job vacancy'. It is such a dirty quotation of yours that you frequently use."

"I know you dislike it when I say about you employing workers, but I think it will do you good."

"Clifford may I remind you of the employees that have worked here over the years and some of the failed interviewees. One man that wanted to work here said 'I'd love to work here but unfortunately I can't read'. Another man volunteered to read fictional books to promote them but what he failed to tell me on his curriculum vitae was that he had a debilitating stutter. I did manage though to employ what I thought would be successful librarians, Mrs Roberts and Mrs Kirby, however, I was wrong again, Mrs Roberts always swiped people's finds, but she only did that to the male customers. She made an agreement that they would pay her in kind if you follow my meaning," said Mr Fickwick winking.

"Oh yes, I forgot about Mrs Roberts and her generous but desperate offers."

"Then there was Mrs Kirby and her unusual phobias."

"They were not that unusual, Mr Fickwick," said Clifford.

"Clifford, the woman was scared of pencils! How is that normal? Not to mention her other phobias like doors, computers, paper clips, spectacles, beards, monks, audio cassettes, prostitutes, bicycle pumps, fat women, skinny women, fat men, skinny men, geeks, dictionaries, thesauruses, gynaecologists, theatres, supermarkets, bingo halls, public transport, amusement parks, kettles, Chinese people, sweat, false teeth, other librarians, academics, tampon machines, lavatories and Christine's mum."

"Wait a minute. This is all very strange, but she was scared of doors? How did she enter and exit this place, even houses or buildings for that matter?"

"She would climb through a window," said Mr Fickwick.

"Crikey, Mr Fickwick. Okay, I see your point now."

"Thank you, Clifford, you have been most helpful." Mr Fickwick put his right hand on Clifford's forehead. "Oh, almighty book king, please guard Clifford Cockflint through his writing expedition. You know his potential, I know his potential, so with your guidance and literary expertise, let them shine brightly within Clifford." Then nothing more was said. He just tapped him on the shoulder and left him to get on with it.

A light switched on in Clifford's head. He thought back to when he was a child, to meeting Christine, them having children, then his relationships with his neighbours. He especially thought about his accident, helping Chris and Christine's cancer. Clifford sat up straight, he leaned forward and started to type. He typed out the first sentence and then could not stop.

Mr Fickwick went into his office to make himself a cup of coffee. He sat down then looked to the other side of the library and watch Clifford type away like a madman. Mr Fickwick held his coffee up high and then said, "God I'm good."

That evening Clifford dropped Chris off at the hospital. Clifford went in as he wanted to speak to Doctor Pukka. He said goodbye to Chris and told him to ring him whenever he needed him or just wanted a conversation. Clifford went to see Doctor Pukka who was in his office speaking to Melvin. "Melvin, how many more times, you cannot call the receptionist fat, it insults her badly."

"Oh, stop overreacting. She is fat, too fat if I have to be honest, and she needs to do something about it."

"You get too personal with the staff, Melvin."

"They are jealous of my good looks," said Melvin.

"Oh, bullocks, Melvin. Just leave now!"

"Okay, okay, I'm going." Melvin left the room just as Clifford was about to walk in.

"Hi, Clifford," said Melvin.

"Hi there, Melvin," replied Clifford.

"Go easy with Doctor P," said Melvin. "He is going through a dramatic menopause," Melvin laughed. Doctor Pukka picked up his clipboard and lobbed it. The clipboard bounced off the door and smacked Melvin on the back of his head.

"Ouch, you always go just that step too far," Melvin whinged, rubbing his sore head.

"Clifford, come in, and shut the door behind you please."

124

Clifford unzipped his coat, put it onto the back of the chair, took a cup from the stand and filled it up with cool, refreshing water.

"Please, Clifford, make yourself at home," said Doctor Pukka sarcastically.

"Doctor Pukka, I have come to tell you about Chris's excellent progress."

"What about his progress?" asked Doctor Pukka.

"Well could you at least sound interested," said Clifford with an icy tone.

"Look, Clifford, could you get to the point. I've been at the hospital all day, I'm very tired and I still have a great deal of work to get through."

Clifford was displeased by the lack of care Doctor Pukka appeared to present towards the children's ward. However, Clifford was not going to take that rubbish from him after all the time he had spent helping Chris build up his confidence. "Do you know what your problem is, Doctor Pukka?"

"Please don't patronise me, Clifford. But since you brought it up, what's my problem?"

"You have a hospital for people of all ages. The children that enter this site every day have so much potential, but they are neglected by the people of high status."

"How dare you accuse me of neglecting the people that we accommodate!"

"Don't interrupt me! I am so thankful for the accident that I endured because it led me down a pathway, and that pathway was a direction for me to help people like Chris. What worries me is that I am due back at work next month after a year's sabbatical to be with my wife, and it kills me inside knowing that if I leave this hospital Chris and other young people won't get the attention that they need."

"Clifford, I assure you that Chris will get the best possible care as always."

"I'm not satisfied by that comment, Doctor," said Clifford.

"Well I'm sorry that you're not happy with what I say, but whether you like it or not I really don't care, Clifford. I allowed you to volunteer at this hospital so don't underestimate my authority.

You were a stranger off the streets. I am a trained doctor of seventeen years, I know what to do."

"Yes, you are a brilliant doctor, I cannot disagree with that. However, I disagree with you knowing what to do when it comes to understanding youngsters like Chris."

"Well, Clifford, if you were that concerned why are you leaving?"

"How dare you, Doctor Pukka, you knew that I was an English teacher. I cannot commit myself to masses of activities as I need to spend time with my wife."

"That is not my problem, Clifford. Now please can you leave as my workload is piling up by the minute."

Clifford, feeling angry and frustrated, got up and left. He had lost all the respect that he originally had for Doctor Pukka, and he loathed him for the way he made Clifford feel guilty for leaving the hospital. Now that he was leaving he feared that all the achievements he had made with Chris would be for nothing.

SEVENTEEN

Rufus and Lydia awoke on the morning of their thirtieth wedding anniversary. The air was sour and outside was dark. Rufus gave Lydia a card that said 'Thirty years of uninterrupted wedded bliss'. Lydia laughed in return. She handed Rufus an anniversary card that she had not even bothered to write anything on. They never bought presents for each other as they agreed it would be a waste of money, however, Lydia was surprised that Rufus took that statement as literally as he had as he never bought her anything for any occasion. Rufus never worked on any birthdays or anniversaries. He still got paid, he made sure of that, otherwise he would never take those days off. Rufus asked Lydia the most depressing question he had ever asked her in the whole of the time they had known each other.

"Lydia, how many years do you think we have left together? Twenty years maybe, thirty years, even longer?"

Lydia was left feeling traumatised by that question. She opened her mouth but nothing came out. Rufus waved his hand in front of her face but she did not bat an eyelid. She had a tendency to get lost in her fantasy world when Rufus hit her with unanswerable questions.

Rufus left Lydia to her own devices while he went downstairs to make himself a cup of coffee and read *The Jewish Chronicle*. He was embarrassed to read that Clifford and Christine had published a celebratory speech about their wedding anniversary. It was a picture of them when they were younger. Rufus knew that Lydia would hate them being in the newspaper. He went over to his briefcase and locked the paper in there, however, he did worry that there might be a copy in every Jewish household. The couple were completely unaware of the surprise anniversary party that Clifford, Christine, Sarah and Simon were planning. The couples had made the plan between them but kept it a secret.

It was still early morning and Clifford and Christine were lying in bed going over the last minor details for the party. If Christine had one talent it was certainly that she was outstanding when it came to organising things. If it hadn't been for her the Feldmans would not be getting a party. She was worried about it going smoothly, but as long as everyone turned up she would be happy. Clifford read back a list to Christine and she would shout 'check' if a task was completed. Christine knew that the party had to be of high quality. The Jewish community was very competitive and Christine knew that she was taking on a challenge when she agreed to organise it.

"Well, Christine," said Clifford, "I don't think you have anything to worry about as you have done everything."

"Are you sure now?" said Christine.

"Christine, we have been through this several times."

"Oh, Clifford, don't exaggerate."

"Well just leave it and let everyone enjoy themselves at the party."

"The only people that I am concerned about is Rufus and Lydia."

"I'm sure they'll have an exciting time."

"I doubt it, especially Lydia knowing that Simon will be there with Sarah."

"Oh come on, Christine! We have gone over this more times than the party checklist."

"Yes, Clifford, but you seem to be forgetting one small minor detail."

"And what small minor detail would that be, dearest?" said Clifford.

"What if during the party Simon miraculously gets his memory back, then what? From what you described to me the other evening he will probably explode and go off on one."

Clifford thought for a moment and realised that Christine had made a point. "Lately, Christine, you always seem to spoil the mood."

Christine got up as she was due at Sarah's house because Simon had hired a large van to get all the food over to the hall. The hall was run by Jewish men and they were unsure about Christine walking in and negotiating about money, but when she said it was for Rufus Feldman the Jewish men nearly bit her hand off as they knew very well that he had tons of money in his bank account.

Sarah was also going over the last few details. Meanwhile Simon was in the kitchen cooking her pancakes. For the past two days Simon has stayed as this new person, and he has spent all his time with Sarah and has taken two weeks off work, and has not even set foot inside a church. In actual fact Simon had not even mentioned church or any form of religion at all. Sarah had really enjoyed the past two days, she felt that she was living a dream, and she was worried that it was going to end. However, Sarah was hidden from the unknown, but as Christine knew the truth she was scared about breaking Sarah's heart so her mouth stayed shut.

"Here we are, love," said Simon, walking in with a stack of pancakes smothered in syrup, Nutella, whipped cream, sugar, lemon juice and strawberries. "Now, Sarah love, would you like a cold glass of apple juice or a pot of hot English tea?"

Sarah thought for a moment. "Could I have a frothy coffee?"

"You most certainly can," said Simon, bowing to her demands. Then the doorbell rang unexpectedly.

"Get that will you, Simon." Sarah's demands towards Simon were getting rather tempestuous, but the new Simon went to open the door thinking that he was making Sarah's life easier. Simon answered the door to Christine who was standing there with a list of things for the party.

"Sarah, we need to go over things."

"What again? Calm down, woman! I now regret putting you in charge."

"I'm sorry, I suppose I am getting rather carried away."

"You have not seemed yourself lately, Christine. When are you starting seeing your patients again, yours truly for example?"

"Well, I miss Michelle and Malcolm very, very much and it's killing me inside that I have not seen them for so long. I need them. I need their company. I need their support."

"And have you spoken to Clifford about this?"

"Yes I have, but you know what he is like when it comes to travelling, he hates it, and refuses to leave the ground. Me on the other hand, I would leave tomorrow."

Sarah went into panic mode. She would have a nervous breakdown if Clifford and Christine left the neighbourhood. "Oh, don't say that, Christine, if things get that bad I'm only next door."

Christine reached out for Sarah's hand and rubbed it gently. "Thank you, Sarah, I really appreciate it, but when all is said and done I need my children."

Sarah knew that there would be nothing she could say that would convince Christine. After a year of Sarah living next door to Christine she had never felt so concerned about her. Normally it would be Christine who was concerned for others. For the rest of the afternoon Christine and Sarah went over the party plans then made their way over to the hall.

Clifford and Simon were wearing their suits. Clifford loved wearing his suit and whenever he got the chance to wear a bow tie and a blazer he was there. Tom Jones was playing in the background. Rufus and Lydia were at home, and the plan was that Christine said she was taking them out to dinner so they would be dressed for the occasion.

Clifford had offered to go and collect the two but Christine in the kindest possible way refused as she did not want anything to go wrong. As always Clifford respected her wishes.

Christine parked her car on the driveway. She beeped the horn but then stopped as she remembered that was one thing Rufus despised. It was a loud, unnecessary sound. Christine got out of her car and knocked on the door. Lydia opened it with her hair in curlers.

"Come in, Christine, we are nearly ready."

Rufus was in the shower. He was not looking forward to dinner as he felt unhappy about the way in which the last meal went when he was at the Cockflints. Christine sat in the living room admiring Rufus's possessions. All around the house Jewish symbols hung on the walls, were on the carpets and Rufus and Lydia only watched Jewish television. Rufus had a portfolio of *The Jewish Chronicle* dating back from when he was a child. Christine was astounded what religious beliefs meant to some people.

Eventually Rufus and Lydia were ready. "Come on then, Christine, what exciting restaurant are we going to then?" said Lydia happily.

"It's a surprise." Christine could not wait to see the look on their faces when everyone shouts 'Surprise'. Suddenly Rufus stopped and bent down.

"Hurry up, Rufus!" said Lydia, "We would like to get there today."

But Rufus did not move.

"Are you okay, Rufus?" asked Lydia. She was actually beginning to worry about him. She heard Rufus making strange sounds.

"Well he can't be masturbating, he has got nothing there to grip."

Rufus continued to make alien-like sounds.

"Rufus?" said Christine. Then as if nothing had happened Rufus stood up straight again.

"Yes, yes, I am okay." With that Rufus grabbed his coat and made a move for the car.

Christine and Lydia looked at each other. "That was strange," said Lydia.

"You're telling me," said Christine, and together they followed after Rufus.

Clifford, Sarah and Simon stood waiting by the door to see when Christine would be driving up to the car park.

"She is taking her time," said Sarah.

"All in good time, my dear," said Clifford. "Mind you, I am a bit surprised myself, we all know what women drivers are like," he continued laughing.

"Oh, Clifford, I'll ignore that comment," said Sarah giggling.

Mr Fickwick came outside. "Sorry, folks, that I cannot stay out here with you fellows. You know I would love to but I need to keep an eye on my library. I have been here for about eighteen minutes and this is the longest time I have been outside the library."

"That doesn't matter," said Sarah.

Mr Fickwick patted her on the head. "What a lovely young girl you are," he said, and went back inside.

"He's a nice man," said Sarah.

"Who, Mr Fickwick? Oh yes, he is a great man with a heart of gold," said Clifford.

Simon looked at his watch. "Who are Rufus and Lydia Feldman again?"

"Simon, I have told you over and over again, they live next door to Clifford."

Simon got confused once again. "No they don't, Sarah, we do."

"Oh, do be quiet."

"So he still gets confused does he?" Clifford whispered.

"Greatly, it's his talent."

Just then a car turned into the car park. "Quick, quick, they're here," shouted Clifford.

The three of them ran into the hall and got everything ready. All Rufus's and Lydia's families were there to join in the celebration. Mr Fickwick was sitting by the bar looking at a television screen. On the screen was a smart device meaning that he could watch the library while he was off the grounds. Clifford stood by the door with party poppers waiting for their entrance. Clifford looked at the DJ and waved his hands in the air indicating for him to stop playing the music.

"Okay, everybody, they are coming," said Clifford.

"What the hell are we doing here?" asked Rufus. "This isn't the restaurant, it's a hall run by my enemies."

"Come in for a minute, I left my purse here earlier," Christine lied.

"What were you doing here, Christine?" asked Rufus, but Christine ignored him and went inside.

"Come on then, Rufus, what harm will five minutes make?" said Lydia, and for the first time she linked her arm to Rufus's and together they walked in as husband and wife.

They were immediately greeted with a cheer. "SURPRISE!" went the entire hall in unison. Rufus and Lydia were blown away by the appearance of so many people. Party poppers exploded with a bang and balloons fell from the ceiling landing on everyone. Lydia was overwhelmed by the entire thing and she started welling up. Rufus was deeply embarrassed with this unexpected turn of events.

Sarah went up to Lydia hugging her lovingly, and she whispered into her ear, "This was all down to Christine's extraordinary planning." Lydia nearly fell to her feet as she was overwhelmed by her kindness. Rufus went over to greet his family. His family were very reserved people and they did not enjoy mingling apart from Rufus's auntie who loved mixing with people. Lydia went over to her mother and father and kissed them.

"Hello, Mum, hello, Dad." People had not seen Lydia this happy for a long time. Rufus was happy also.

"Christine, I knew you would be behind all this."

"Oh, Rufus, relax will you and enjoy yourself. Don't worry about the cost of anything, it has all been taken care of."

Rufus slumped back onto a chair. "Oh, thank the rabbi," he said with a sigh of relief.

"Come to the bar, Rufus, and I'll get you a drink," said Clifford as he put his arm around him.

Christine and Sarah sat talking about how happy Lydia was, but when Sarah took a look at Simon he looked dazed and surprised. He seemed like a toddler looking for his mother in a shop.

"Earth to Simon, Earth to Simon," said Sarah, but Simon did nothing except stare at Lydia.

"Simon, will you go over and talk to Lydia if you're going to stare at her like that." Christine felt a little nervous and she pondered whether or not Simon's memory was in the process of returning. Unfortunately for Christine Simon's memory was returning, and memories of the night he spent with Lydia were flooding back. He shook his head while rubbing his eyes.

"Sarah, I'll go and get Simon a drink." Christine ran quickly to get Clifford.

Clifford, Rufus and Mr Fickwick were at the bar having a laugh and reminiscing about their younger years.

"My goodness, it is strange to think that it was thirty years ago today that I smashed that glass at my wedding," said Rufus.

Clifford was dumbfounded by this comment. "What a stupid place to leave a glass, and on the floor of all places where you were getting married. That is so dangerous. You were lucky that you did not end up in hospital and having a doctor remove pieces of glass from your foot."

Rufus could not believe that a man like Clifford that had such intelligence could say the most ridiculous things. "No, no, Clifford, I don't think you understand. I was supposed to step on the glass and smash it with my right foot. It's a Jewish tradition during a wedding service you see."

"Are you being serious, Rufus? Wouldn't it be easier and safer to step on a plastic cup?"

"Clifford, I don't get to decide the rituals, Jewish people always smash a glass. In theory is it unknown how this idea was created, but personally I believe that it symbolises a long-lasting and happy marriage with your new bride."

Clifford thought Rufus was having a joke. "Crikey! A happy marriage? How much of that glass did you smash?"

This grabbed Mr Fickwick's attention. "He chipped it," he said, subtly pointing at Rufus.

"Yes, thank you, Mr Fickwick," said Rufus displeased.

Finally a panic stricken Christine located Clifford and without thinking she grabbed his arm and whispered into his ear. "Clifford, disaster is about to strike. You need to come right away."

"Is it that important?" said Clifford, sipping his J20. Christine leant into him, "Simon's memory is returning." Clifford nearly choked on his drink and spat it out over Christine. Rufus and Mr Fickwick were bewildered but just ignored the situation when suddenly Rufus's pain started to come back again.

"Simon, are you okay?" asked Clifford. "Come outside for a moment." Clifford and Christine took Simon outside for a bit of fresh air. Sarah stood outside and watched what was going on.

"It's okay, Sarah, love, we'll take it from here," said Christine. "I'll talk to him as if I was conducting a session." Sarah felt happier when she said that so she went back inside.

Clifford held Simon up in front of a bush. "Simon, Simon, talk to me." Clifford was slapping his face then he did it again. "This is really good fun."

"Clifford stop it!" said Christine.

"I'm sorry."

Simon was struggling to form properly structured sentences. His brain was going through his memories in chronological order. Then he fell backwards into the bush.

"Come on then, Christine, we might as well leave him there."

"Don't you dare, Clifford!"

Sarah was waiting for them to go back in. She felt that she had been waiting for too long so she went outside to see what the problem was. Simon lay in the bush, and it appeared that he was unconscious as he was not moving. Clifford and Christine stood there contemplating what was the best thing for them to do. Sarah let out a scream, "Oh, my goodness, what has happened to my Simon?"

"Sarah, you will not believe this but I think Simon has had another vision." Clifford knew that Sarah would not believe it this time.

"Lydia, Lydia," Simon muttered lying in the bushes.

"He is calling for Lydia." Sarah felt confused. "Why would he be calling for Lydia?"

"Well," said Christine, "everyone in the hall did just shout 'Lydia' so maybe he is having some kind of dreaming fit."

"Exactly, Christine, your right," said Clifford reassuring his wife.

Sarah knelt down beside Simon. "Come on, Simon, I'll take you home."

Clifford and Christine were relieved at the prospect of Sarah taking him home. "Well, if it's for the best," said Clifford.

"Yes, Rufus and Lydia would understand, they definitely would understand." Clifford helped Simon to the car. "Now, Sarah, make sure you get Simon home and into bed."

"Yes I will, Clifford, do you think I need to call a doctor?"

"No, certainly not, I think he would just say you're wasting his time."

"Okay then," said Sarah sighing. Then she drove away from the party leaving Clifford and Christine standing outside. The minute Sarah turned the corner and disappeared into the night the pair of them jumped up in the air to have their own little celebration.

"Oh, Clifford, I thought she would never take Simon home."

"Oh crumbs, love, feel my heart. I was on the brink of having a heart attack."

The pair of them held hands and went back into the hall to join in the party. Christine went to sit with Lydia and her parents while Clifford went back to Rufus and Mr Fickwick.

"Well thank you for coming," said Rufus sarcastically.

"Sorry, I had a personal emergency to attend to."

As the night continued more and more people were dancing and laughing out loud. Not a single person seemed to be bored.

Rufus's pain progressively became worse and his chest was tightening. Clifford and Mr Fickwick were laughing about the time they thought a ghost was in the library making noises, but it turned out to be an escaped tiger who had escaped from the zoo and snuck in through the back door. Rufus went into a corner and struggled to stand up straight. Clifford watched Rufus go. "Oi, where do you think you are going you party pooper?"

Rufus's hearing had become muffled by the sound. Suddenly he thought he was deaf as there was no noise. He could not hear any music being played. Clifford for the second time became distressed by another person.

"Mr Fickwick, what is Rufus doing?"

Mr Fickwick stared at Rufus worryingly. "Oh my word, I think I could be wrong but I think he is having a heart attack." No sooner had Mr Fickwick finished his sentence than Rufus collapsed to the floor. Clifford and Mr Fickwick ran to his aid.

"Crikey, Clifford, we need to call an ambulance," said Mr Fickwick. The pair of them carried Rufus out into a quieter room. Luckily there was a sofa which they laid him on.

Christine happened to walk past. She assumed nothing but when she investigated more her concerns grew. Clifford had laid Rufus on the sofa in a manner so that he was comfortable, and Mr Fickwick checked to make sure that he was still breathing which he was. Christine barged in but when she saw the state that Clifford was in she said nothing.

"The ambulance is on its way," said Mr Fickwick."

"Who is going to tell Lydia?" said Clifford. The pair of them looked at Christine. "I think it would be right coming from you, love," said Clifford.

Christine said nothing. She was just worried about Rufus, so she went to find Lydia. Ironically Lydia was happy and having fun dancing with her family until she saw the deathly appearance on Christine's face.

Lydia entered the room and saw her husband lying helplessly on the sofa with all life and hope draining from his body. Clifford, Christine and Mr Fickwick stepped back sorrowfully. Christine lay her head on Clifford's shoulder and felt tearful. Mr Fickwick, even though he was tempted to check how his library was, actually turned off the screen as a mark of respect. Lydia began to cry realising that she had let Rufus down and was thinking that she did love him very much. The sudden prospect of losing him hit her hard and she knew that she needed him around. Lydia started kissing his face praying that he would not die. Rufus just laid there oblivious to everything.

The next morning Lydia was driving home. The clouds were dark and only the car's headlights could be seen through the thick fog. "How was I to know that I was suffering from heartburn?" said Rufus, who sat in the back seat of the car resting.

Lydia who was relieved that Rufus was going to be okay still felt embarrassed that she worried as badly as she did. "Rufus, you worried everyone, and all because you had heartburn," she said rolling her eyes.

"But the doctor said it was severe," said Rufus, who was trying to make it sound worse than it actually was.

"Oh, Rufus, I don't believe it," Lydia smiled. She could not stay angry for long. During the night Lydia had to wait in the waiting room for hours, and during that time she re-evaluated her marital status. She believed that this sudden attack on Rufus made her realise just how much she loved him, and luckily she was given a second chance to make up her relationship with him. Regarding her one-night fling with Simon, she had decided not to think about it again and pretended that it never happened. She thought that what Rufus did not know would never haunt him. Lydia pulled up on the driveway. The area had an eerie silence and she turned and looked directly into Rufus's eyes. "Listen, Rufus, I have to be honest with you. When I thought you were having a heart attack, straight away I imagined my life without you. At first I thought maybe it would be better if you just slipped away quietly…"

Rufus felt insulted. "Well, thanks very much."

"No, but this is my point, Rufus. I realised that I could not imagine my life in the future without you."

Rufus had never felt so loved by his wife and he respected her for her honesty. The problems that had occurred over the years felt like they had finally come to an end. Rufus and Lydia felt that they could finally move on.

"Lydia, I know that in the past I have been a bit of a nightmare husband, and I may have said some rather hurtful things, but I really do love you and appreciate you very much." For once something that Rufus said did not have an unkind attachment to it. The tone of his voice and the look in his eyes spelt out meaningful honesty.

"Oh, Rufus, you have no idea how long I have waited to hear you say that."

They started kissing then her back clicked and Rufus got cramp in his leg. "Ouch!" they said in unison.

"Now, Lydia Feldman, let's go in the house and decide which parts need to be redecorated and what old things need to be binned," said Rufus rubbing his leg hoping that the pain would go away.

"Are you being serious, Rufus? But that means spending money. What happened to your strict Jewish rules?"

"Forget my old past, this is the new me!" Rufus spoke with pride and happiness. Lydia said nothing and agreed. Rufus wanted to be romantic and carried Lydia into the house, but his back was not as strong as what it was, so together they walked hand in hand and went into the house to start their new life.

Simon watched from the downstairs window Lydia and Rufus walk happily into their house. Simon realised that the best way to overcome this problem was to forget what he did, forget the one-night stand. He knew that if he and Sarah had decided to move then it would never come up in conversation, that dreadful and mind lingering memory of him and Lydia at it and probably disturbing the moles that lived in the ground. Simon looked into the mirror. He looked tired and overworked. "I am doing the right thing, moving to a new house and leaving people behind. Of course Lydia would be at the wedding, but that would be it. Moving will help, won't it? No one will ever find out... will they?"

EIGHTEEN

Clifford was driving Chris back to the hospital after spending an afternoon at the library. Chris was quiet as he sat miserably in the passenger seat. Clifford knew that Chris would be unhappy as he could not adjust to change easily. "Clifford, why do you have to leave?"

"I need to go back to my job at the school. When I took time off it was agreed that I would return and go back a year later. I just cannot go back on my word."

There was silence.

"Oh, em, Chris, about what you told me the other day about your parents leaving you and driving away. Thanks for sharing that with me."

"It's okay, Clifford, I trust you. It was difficult for me to relive that memory."

"I understand, Chris."

"No you don't!" snapped Chris. "If you understood you would not leave."

"Wait a minute, Chris. Now that's not fair."

There was silence.

Clifford was aware that all this was upsetting Chris but there was nothing he could do. Clifford's worst thought was Chris comparing him to his parents. His parents dropped him off at the psychiatric hospital and never went back, Clifford was positive that this was what Chris was thinking. They approached the hospital then they walked in together for the last time.

"Chris you can still call me whenever you want... after five though."

"But there will be no point calling you then. I will just ask Nurse May for something."

Clifford helped Chris into his room. They had one more conversation then the time had come for Clifford to leave. Chris said goodbye and he knew that his friendship with Clifford was at an end. Clifford stood in the doorway and watched Chris choose a book off his shelf. He got settled then Clifford left feeling empty and alone. As he walked down the hallway Doctor Pukka came out of his office. "So you really are leaving then?" he said smirking.

"Go away, Doctor Pukka," said Clifford turning his head away. Clifford pushed open the door and left the hospital without saying goodbye to anyone. "So this is how my book is going to end. My expectations certainly did not envisage this."

Doctor Pukka watched Clifford drive out of the car park till he disappeared into the distance. He smiled. "He'll be back," he said to himself.

The alarm went off with a shrill sound on that cold Monday morning. Clifford rose from his bed tired but ready to start his day back at school. Christine had laid his suit on the chair in their bedroom. Clifford had a quick shower followed by a hot cup of tea which he always had before he started his day. Still feeling guilty about leaving Chris in the hospital, he went downstairs put his coat on and went to pick up Rufus.

"Good morning, sir," said Rufus jokingly. Since his house was having a complete makeover this had changed Rufus's attitude. Suddenly to him every day was a great day.

"Good morning, Rufus, are you sure that you are ready to go back to school?"

"Ready?" said Rufus. "I for one am more than ready." The new optimism that Rufus had adopted did him a massive favour.

Clifford started the car and he and Rufus made their way down the normal route to work. Clifford was curious as to how long Rufus could keep his happy personality up.

"How are you and Lydia getting on these days?" enquired Clifford.

"Oh, Clifford, we are getting on brilliantly. It's so fantastic. Ever since my near death experience we have learnt to accept each other."

"Near death experience? More like the exaggerated pain in the chest," said Clifford mockingly.

"Yes, yes, Clifford, I know. I have had no sympathy from anyone but I really was in excruciating pain." Rufus was fed up that everyone was laughing at him for only suffering from bad chest pains. Even Mr Fickwick when he was conducting a presentation at the library made his audience laugh like a pack of wild monkeys because they all thought it was utterly hilarious, but Rufus was not going to break his happy and sound mood.

The sound of loud schoolchildren could be heard for miles. Clifford approached some children who were messing about bicycling along the road. He steered away from them but Rufus would not stand for any of their nonsense, and all of a sudden his new attitude had vanished. He shouted out of the window, "You three, stop that stupidity at once, because if you get knocked off your bicycles you will have only yourselves to blame!" Rufus had an annoying voice that changed dramatically when he was trying to shout over noise.

Next Clifford drove past some teenagers in their last year smoking in a group. Once again this was behaviour that Rufus did not tolerate. "Put those cigarettes away otherwise I will ring your parents and tell them that you cannot be trusted to walk to school together without putting dirty cigarettes in your mouths!"

The teenagers made rude hand gestures at the window and shouted unpleasant things at him. "Piss off, you wanker!" shouted one of the students.

Rufus was horrified. "Oh my goodness, Clifford, stop the car, stop the car right now!"

"Rufus, there are buses behind me and those kids have run off now."

"Those annoying children," Rufus grumped.

Clifford and Rufus entered the school grounds. Rufus had already run off shouting at some children that he was dissatisfied with. Clifford was greeted with, "Hello, sir, welcome back," and, "It's nice to see you, sir. Is Mrs Cockflint feeling better now?" Clifford was overwhelmed by the students but as he stood there and watched the children get on with whatever they were doing, he wondered whether or not the hospital needed him more than the students of this school.

The school bell rang indicating to the students that lessons were beginning. Clifford went into the staffroom to get twenty-nine copies of *Frankenstein* out of his locker and bring them to his class. Clifford had a little laugh to himself thinking that if Mr Fickwick could see him carrying twenty-nine copies of the same book he would say, 'Oh I see you're keen to read it more than once'.

Clifford got a cheer from the class as he walked in. "Good morning, class, Mr Cockflint is back and ready to teach you young whippersnappers all about Mary Shelley's brilliant and one of my favourite novels, *Frankenstein.*" As he handed out the copies of the novel Clifford was explaining a background summary of the author's life. Already he was aware that the students were becoming uninterested with the topic. Clifford called for attention, then he blew his whistle and made up his mind. The class fell silent and waited for Clifford's response. "As from next term I will no longer be a teacher at this school. I am going to work in a hospital and help children who need me there."

The class were stunned by this speech. "Why, sir, why are you leaving? You have only just come back," said Sophie the spotty girl who sat at the back of the room.

"That is a very good question indeed, Sophie. I am leaving because there are teenagers who need my help more in a completely different environment. I volunteered to work there while I was on my leave, and quite frankly I have never enjoyed a job as much as I did then."

When the bell went Clifford dismissed his class. He wasted no time and he locked his classroom door then marched straight into Rufus's office. He interrupted Rufus lecturing two students on why it was dangerous to make paper aeroplanes and that if they cut themselves with the paper the cut could become infected. Clifford asked for a resigning sheet then sat at the table and wrote a two-page letter of resignation. Rufus had finally stopped shouting at the two students. "Why, when you run like that outside, what if some helpless person was looking for a member of staff and carelessly tripped over your legs, fell and damaged the concrete? I for one would not be happy."

Clifford put the letter on his desk. Rufus quickly glanced at it and just the word resignation grabbed his attention. "Clifford, you're leaving us?" said Rufus unsurprised in the least.

"Yes, Rufus, I am sorry but I have made up my mind." Clifford had the tone of a war general.

"Well I am not going to try to stop you, Clifford. From the moment you left that hospital you have been miserable. Now go and get your duties back from the hospital and show Doctor Pukka how to do his job."

Clifford had never felt this inspired by Rufus in all the years that he had known him and he was happy by this. When the school day was finished Clifford got into his car, dropped Rufus home and drove straight to the hospital to demand his voluntary job back.

At the hospital all was quiet. The nurses were getting on with their jobs and Doctor Pukka and Melvin were arguing as usual. When Clifford burst through the door everybody knew about it. The receptionist was so pleased to see him. "Hello, everyone," said Clifford. He got into the elevator and pressed the button which would bring him to level six which was the floor that Doctor Pukka was on. Doctor Pukka and Melvin's conversation was interrupted by the sound of Clifford demanding his job back. Clifford's face was as red as a tomato. He was sweaty and his speech was hard to understand as he was panting for dear life.

"Well, well, well, look who comes crawling back," Doctor Pukka sniggered, secretly happy to see Clifford.

"Listen, Doctor, I know that we have grown to hate each other, but the fact is I love this hospital and I am willing to leave my job to be here. I do not care if I don't get paid but I want to stay here with Chris and the others. What do you say?"

Doctor Pukka picked up his glass of water and slowly drank it. "I understand you want to visit your children at Christmas?" said Doctor Pukka randomly.

Clifford was taken aback. "Yes, that is correct, but how did you know that?"

"Chris told me that you and your wife have not seen your children for some time."

"Yes, we miss them terribly," said Clifford looking at the floor.

"Right, I take it you cannot leave your teaching job until the Christmas holidays?"

"Yes, that is right. What's your point?"

"Clifford, I am being nice to you. I have learnt today that the students worship you. So at Christmas have that long month visiting your children, then come back to the hospital completely refreshed and start the job from new."

Clifford was overwhelmed by Doctor Pukka's unexpected kindness and generosity. A tear rolled down his cheek. "Oh, Doctor Pukka, you will not regret this."

"Listen, Clifford, I am not normally this kind, so when you get back expect to be doing fifteen-hour shifts." Doctor Pukka forgot all the times he and Clifford had small disagreements and only thought ahead.

Clifford started laughing. "Doctor Pukka, I will work all hours." On that note Clifford left, happily ready to take anything that the world was ready to throw at him.

"Doctor Pukka," said Melvin wearily.

"What, Melvin?" he answered.

"Can I have a holiday? Its six years since my last one." Melvin's sounded like an unhappy child.

"Forget it, Melvin, you're the only person who is not entitled to a holiday."

"That's not fair. However, my last three bosses said that to me as well. I am this really annoying person that everybody hates."

"Well under the circumstances which making it officially unofficial within the clockwise sense of the time which you in all probability fail to meet will stop you from the indulgence privilege of experiencing."

"What?" said Melvin in a childlike tone.

"Melvin, while I am in charge of this hospital you will never have a holiday!"

Chris was at the library with Mr Fickwick and Clifford did not have the time to tell him the good news about his return. Even if he wanted to telephone the library Mr Fickwick never answered the phone during his working hours. Clifford knew that he still had a duty of being the best possible teacher for his last remaining weeks there teaching his unenthusiastic students. Rufus was worried that Miss Nice, the teacher that was not nice, would return, as were the

144

students, but there was nothing they could do that would change Clifford's mind. When Clifford got home he rang Chris and left a message telling him that after Christmas he would working at the hospital. While he was leaving a message Lydia was upstairs speaking to Christine about the new lifestyle she was living.

"Oh Christine, I cannot tell you how happy the past few days have been for me. Rufus is a new person, and let me tell you something that will surprise you. There are builders all over the house redecorating and completely turning the house upside down." Lydia continued to talk uncontrollably. She could not stop herself.

Christine thought to herself, I knew I should have bought myself a laptop. It would have made my life so much easier. Christine always said that a change in lifestyle will change a person, and now that Rufus had seen the light and changed his ways it had made a massive impact on Lydia's life. Suddenly Lydia's mood swings had calmed down and Christine was saving money as she was not spending so much on tissues, and she was saving time by not having to clear up the mess of tissues which covered her office when Lydia left at the end of each session.

"Well, Lydia, I have to say that I feel relaxed leaving to visit Malcolm and Michelle knowing that you're a lot happier now."

"Oh, I am, Christine, I really am."

"Well don't you go and ruin this now by sleeping with Simon..." Christine stopped herself speaking as she realised that she had put herself in an awkward situation. Lydia was horrified knowing that if Rufus found out this happiness that she was finally living could come to an end.

"Oh no, Christine, so that husband of yours finally told you. He promised me, Christine, Clifford promised me that he would be discreet about my silly mistake."

"Lydia, Lydia, I am really sorry... so has Rufus changed the bedroom?" said Christine, trying to change the subject as she did not want to make a big thing of Lydia's and Simon's one-night mistake. Plus she knew that Clifford had told her in the strictest confidence.

"Wait until I see your husband! I will kill him! Sarah must never know about this."

However, Christine stopped worrying about what Clifford would say when she remembered the stupidity of what Clifford and Lydia cooked up to explain to Sarah Simon's sudden change of life. "But, Lydia, you told Sarah that he had a vision from an angel. Don't you realise that one day Simon will remember. He could remember right now for all we know."

"Christine, please. I was happy for a change during these sessions and now you, who is supposed to help me see the better side of life, have done everything backwards."

"I am sorry once again, Lydia. I did not plan to mention this, however, since I have let's talk about it. Why? Lydia, is the first thing that comes to my mind. How could you do this to Sarah? We are meant to be close friends, so how could you even look her directly in the face?"

Stubbornness was written all over Lydia's face. She detested being questioned about things she hated talking about. Unfortunately for her when it came to Christine's job she was not a soft touch and she pushed Lydia for answers.

"Okay, Christine, what I did was unforgiveable, I know that, but since that night I have lived with the guilt, but I cannot go back with what has happened."

"Have you spoken to Simon since?" enquired Christine.

"No, I have not seen him, but then again when did we ever see him?"

"That's true, Lydia, but you will see him eventually. I mean the wedding is not that far away."

"I know but I will forget about what happened as I am sure that you and Clifford will do also, and enjoy what is meant to be the happiest day of Sarah's life."

"Yes, you're right, Lydia." Then Christine said quietly, "In order to protect Sarah she must never ever know about you and Simon, as I am sure if Simon remembers he will never tell her because of the thought of losing her, and also the laws of his religion about sex outside of marriage and adultery."

Lydia said that if Sarah ever found out about this that it would not have come from her, and Christine promised for the sake of Sarah that it would be kept a secret.

PART THREE

NINETEEN

THREE MONTHS LATER...

Friday morning and the airport was busy. Thousands of people were scurrying to the small coach that took the passengers to their plane. Businessmen in suits were sitting catching up with the *Financial Times*, mothers were purchasing sweets for their children who were feeling hyper about going on holiday and fathers were making last-minute phone calls. Pilots went into the small shops to get bottles of alcohol and caffeine pills to keep them going, and one pilot was reading a book called *How to Fly an Aeroplane*. Celebrities wore sunglasses and hurried through the airport trying to be inconspicuous. Some managed to successfully stay hidden. Brian Blessed got caught by the public just by sneezing. The cast of *Red Dwarf* tried to stay hidden but their exuberant costumes and a crew carrying a spaceship through the airport did not help their wishes of privacy. Cleaners were laboriously sweeping the floors then taking two-hour breaks by sitting on their trollies reading the latest gossip magazines. The queues for McDonald's seemed to go on for miles and the workers in the back were having heart palpitations as screaming customers were demanding their food. The announcer of the airport obviously liked the sound of her voice as she constantly made pointless announcements. "The last plane going to California will be leaving. Can Jackie please come to the staffroom, that's Jackie to the staffroom. Thank you. Did anybody watch *EastEnders* last night? It ended with an interesting cliffhanger. In my magazine this girl called Sophie has been seeing a married man with four kids and now she is pregnant. Blimey, what is happening in this modern world?" This was an ordinary day at the airport.

Christine sat on a metal chair with her and Clifford's luggage around them. She sat with her legs crossed drinking a cup of coffee and figuring out a quite challenging crossword. Clifford came out of the toilet for the third time and joined Christine. His entire body was shaking and he found it difficult to string two sentences together. Christine stopped and rested her hand on Clifford's leg. "Stop worrying."

"Will you stop saying that! The more you repeat it, the more it will not affect me," said Clifford.

"Once we are sitting comfortably on the plane all your worries will have disappeared," said Christine trying desperately to calm him down.

"Christine, I am not one of your dysfunctional patients," said Clifford, who got very snappy when nervous.

"Clifford, please refrain from bringing my patients into this."

"Sorry, Christine. Yes, that was out of order."

Christine carried on with the crossword and Clifford just sat there in silence but not for long. "Strange, isn't it?" said Clifford.

"What is?" replied Christine.

"For the past few weeks I have not seen Simon or Sarah. Have you?" asked Clifford.

Christine thought for a moment. She had a tendency to tap the end of her chin with her pencil when deep in thought. Clifford knew when she was thinking or concentrating because her pencil would be bouncing off her chin. "My word, Clifford, you're right. I have not seen either of them for a while. Sarah cancelled our session four weeks ago and she never did rebook, plus she has not been round for a morning coffee with Lydia and I."

"Oh crumbs, I hope they are both okay," said a genuinely concerned Clifford.

"I am sure they are. I doubt Simon and Sarah have eloped together."

They both started laughing.

"True, true," giggled Clifford.

"So how long do you think Rufus will keep his kind man act up?" asked Clifford.

"Not for much longer," said Christine. "Only last week I thought he was going to crack."

"Why, what did he do?"

"He allowed Lydia to buy some cushions," Christine replied.

"And Rufus was feeling okay? He has only just paid for the house refurbishments."

"Well, like I said, I cannot see it lasting."

"I do give Rufus credit though. Mr Fickwick and I made a bet that he would not last two weeks, but he has."

"How is Mr Fickwick? I have not seen him since Rufus's and Lydia's anniversary."

"Mr Fickwick is preposterously mad as a hatter but he's a fantastic. His encouragement on my writing is incredible. He has a talent for building up confidence within people. I mean take Chris for example, he has really come on board with people and communication. I am really pleased."

"I am pleased with you, Clifford," said Christine lovingly.

"Why?" said Clifford.

"You manage to always be the same person no matter what happens. Your accident was very traumatic but you still carry on being yourself."

"One gets used to things," said Clifford reminiscing about the nudists in the field. "I have you by my side, Christine. You're the light in me that keeps me alive."

"Oh, Clifford," said Christine giggling. She leant in for a kiss as did Clifford.

"I love you, Christine."

"I love you, Clifford."

Then a scruffy bald man in a crumpled suit turned around holding an empty plastic cup. "Can you two stop that! I can feel my cappuccino coming back up."

Clifford and Christine looked at the man's red face and both sat back up straight, with Christine continuing to finish her challenging crossword and Clifford going back to shaking like a nervous leaf.

The announcer caught the passengers' attention. "All passengers flying to New York please make your way over to door three please. I repeat, will all passengers flying to New York make your way over to door three. That's door three. Thank you." The couple gathered all their luggage together and made their way to door three.

Clifford and Christine were sitting on the aeroplane waiting for take-off. There was not a cloud in the sky and the people on the plane seemed pleasant. So far everything was going smoothly. Clifford sat there shaking like a leaf dangling on an old dead tree being blown by the wind. Christine put her hand on his. "Calm down, Clifford, once we get in the air everything will be fine."

Christine's words were not helping him. "Why just when we are flying in the air? Will we not be fine taking off?" said Clifford panting. It seemed as if he was going to have an extreme panic attack.

"No, no, no, Clifford, I am just saying that it seems the plane is not moving once we are in the air."

"Okay, okay, I'm fine, I'm fine." Clifford felt that his appearance had aged ten years since being on the plane. What is worse? he thought. If he had felt that he had aged ten years and the plane had not even started moving, he dreaded his appearance when the plane landed in New York. He worried about being a dead ringer for a dead corpse of about one hundred years, or just looking as old as Dolly Parton.

"I cannot believe Simon and Sarah are moving," said Christine changing the subject.

"Really? You're surprised? I'm not. Poor Simon cannot handle the guilt of looking out of his window every day and seeing Lydia and then seeing our front garden and knowing that he knocked a dozen of his sperm out in one go."

"I suppose when you put it like that," said Christine trying to get that image out of her head. The captain made his regular speech about the duration of the flight then the aeroplane started. Clifford squeezed Christine's hand until it went purple.

"Argh, Clifford, you're hurting me!"

"Why did we have children? We would not be going through this."

"Stop it, Clifford," said Christine.

The aeroplane got faster and faster and soon was high in the sky. Clifford had lost his sense of fear and was now sitting comfortably in his seat playing games with Christine.

While another game was loading the couple carried on with their conversation. "In a way, Clifford, I am glad we are not home this week."

"Why is that, my love?" said Clifford who was flicking through the duty free magazine.

"Mr and Mrs Dippy are having their house demolished."

"What! Mr and Mrs Dippy? Don't they live at number sixteen?"

"Yes, that's right."

Clifford was aghast. "But number sixteen is a gorgeous little house that overlooks the street."

"I know but it is up to them. They're away this week too," said Christine.

"Christine, we are lucky," said Clifford.

"Yes, Clifford, we are."

"I mean here we are on an aeroplane and travelling to New York to see our children, then returning home and I am starting a new and satisfying job. What could be any better?"

"It will just be us and our kids for the next two weeks. Perfect."

Now and then the air hostesses brought round tea and coffee for the passengers. Everything was calm and happy and the plane was flying at a steady pace. Clifford and Christine could not have felt any happier. They had been flying for about three hours so far.

Two men in building gear were walking along Castle Avenue trying to read a letter. The letter was a crumpled sheet of paper and the top half on the sheet had a rip in it. "Barry, how did you manage to rip this letter?"

"Sorry, boss, it got caught in the door and I pulled it which caused the rip."

"Barry, this letter had vital information on it." The boss angrily crunched the paper into a ball and threw it. "Now what are we going to do?" said the boss as he buried his head in his hands.

"Boss, why don't we just call Mr Dippy?" said Barry, thinking he was helping.

"Barry, you ignoramus! Don't you think I would have done that by now if I could? They're on holiday. This is why Mrs Dippy trusted this company because I guaranteed her that her house would be absolutely safe in our care." The boss and Barry walked up and down the street examining the houses but when they got outside Clifford's and Christine's house they decided to stop and rest. They both leant on the fence like alley cats.

At that point Rufus came out with his wheelie bin and put it on his driveway ready for the dustbin lorry to empty it. He noticed the two builders standing there. "Excuse me, gents, they're not in, the owners of the house have gone on holiday."

The boss and Barry looked at each other. "Thank you, sir," shouted the boss, "you have saved us a lot of trouble."

"No problem," said Rufus. He waved acknowledging what he said then went back inside.

The boss took out his mobile phone from his work jacket. "Okay, Tony, I have located Mr and Mrs Dippy's house. Could you bring the wrecking ball now please?" The boss hung up. "Tony is bring the wrecking ball around now," he said to Barry.

"It's a shame," said Barry.

"What are you talking about now, Barry?" said the boss.

"That someone would want to destroy this lovely house."

The boss looked at the house realising that Barry had made a good point. "That's very true, Barry, but you know what this generation is like. We always want the new."

The demolition lorry arrived with the wrecking ball. It was enormous and was ready for destroying. The boss walked up to the driver. "Okay, Tony, let's start now before it gets dark."

Tony stuck his head out of the driver's window. He glared at the house then smiled. "Let's rip down this house."

A taxi was travelling with a male and female sitting in the back. The taxi was about three miles away from Castle Avenue. Three suitcases were in the boot of the car. The boy took some money out of his wallet. "There you are, sir," he said handing it to the taxi driver. "I have to pay for it now otherwise my parents will and I don't want them to." The man and woman who were sitting in the taxi were young. The girl looked as if she was in her twenties as did the boy.

"Malcolm, I cannot wait to see the look on Mum's and Dad's faces when they open the door."

"You're right, Michelle, this was a brilliant idea of agreeing to turn up out of the blue as a surprise," said Malcolm.

"Well, we have not seen them for such a long time, so I thought it would nice if we turned up now, and just in time for Christmas too."

"Yes, we got lucky. If we were in New York now there would not be any flights home until after the New Year, and that is the same for Australia too."

Together Malcolm and Michelle sat in excitement looking forward to seeing the look on their parents' faces. "I see Simon and Sarah have not being around for a while. Dad told me on the phone last week," said Malcolm.

"And there were builders in Rufus's house doing work in their front room," said Michelle. "I think we have been away for too long," she continued. Suddenly they heard a loud slamming sound. "Did you hear that?" asked Michelle listening with her head outside the window.

"Some construction work must be going on near Mum and Dad's house," Malcolm replied.

Michelle was tired after a long day of travelling and she yawned. She looked at her watch. "It's four thirty. Right, Malcolm, when we get there shall I knock and surprise them?"

THE END

Printed in Great Britain
by Amazon.co.uk, Ltd.,
Marston Gate.